The Good, the Bad & the Beagle

CATHERINE LLOYD BURNS

The Good, the Bad & the Beagle

FARRAR STRAUS GIROUX
New York

For Red Burns and Fanny Gennis

Farrar Straus Giroux Books for Young Readers
175 Fifth Avenue, New York 10010

Printed in the United States of America
by RR Donnelley & Sons Company, Harrisonburg, Virginia
First edition, 2014
1 3 5 7 9 10 8 6 4 2

mackids.com

Library of Congress Cataloging-in-Publication Data
Burns, Catherine Lloyd.
The good, the bad, and the beagle / Catherine Lloyd Burns.
pages cm
Summary: Shy, eleven-year-old Veronica Louise Morgan of New York City is not happy about having to attend Randolf School for Girls, but by the end of her first year she not only has some new friends, she may have finally convinced her parents that she is ready to own a dog.
ISBN 978-0-374-30039-5 (hardback)
ISBN 978-0-374-30040-1 (e-book)
[1. Dogs—Fiction. 2. Family life—New York (State)—New York—Fiction. 3. Schools—Fiction. 4. Friendship—Fiction. 5. New York (N.Y.)—Fiction. 6. Humorous stories.] I. Title.

PZ7.B9364Goo 2014
[Fic]—dc23

2014010848

Farrar Straus Giroux Books for Young Readers may be purchased for business or promotional use. For information on bulk purchases please contact Macmillan Corporate and Premium Sales Department at (800) 221-7945 x5442 or by e-mail at specialmarkets@macmillan.com.

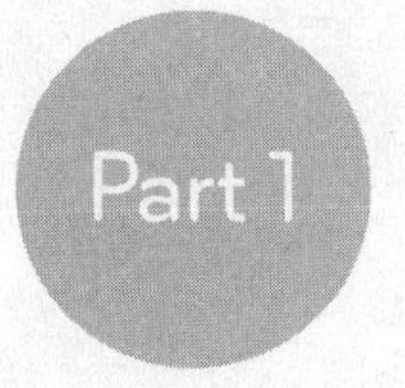
Part 1

An Alphabet of Woes

There was a patch of dry, scaly skin on Veronica Louise Morgan's left middle finger that she hated. Scratching was useless because the itch was below the bone. The only thing that helped was rubbing her knuckle back and forth against the green carpet in her bedroom until the whole thing was numb. She'd been rubbing her finger this way for twenty minutes already and the clock by her bed read 7:05 a.m.

Today was her first day at the Randolf School for Girls.

She would never survive.

The sounds of the coffee grinder and the front door closing infuriated her. This meant her father had just brought in the newspaper and her mother was making breakfast. Didn't the last day of their eleven-year-old daughter's life deserve some kind of ceremony instead of business as usual?

"Honey, what kind of bagel do you want?" her mother called. Veronica rubbed her knuckle harder. Her family was incredible. Who could think of things like bagels at a time like this?

The rug burned through more layers of skin while the aroma of sweet, warm, yeasty bread wafting from the kitchen made Veronica's mouth water. She pushed images of yellow butter collecting in foamy pools along the surface of a lightly toasted bagel right out of her mind.

"Sesame," she called. Oh well. She might as well enjoy one last breakfast.

"What?" her mother called back.

"Sesame!"

"Veronica, don't shout!"

Ordinarily, Veronica Morgan would be very happy to point out that her mother was the person doing the shouting, but this being the last day of her life and all, she didn't have the wherewithal to fight. She had some sense of decency, unlike the people she lived with.

"Veronica, Daddy and I are *dying* to see you in your *uniform*! Hurry up!"

Oh God. How could she ever leave her room? The only advice the twelfth-grade Randolf tour guide had given her was regarding uniform length. The girl's name was Lynn Dehavenon and Lynn Dehavenon said uniforms had to be seven inches above the knee. That was the protocol for girls who were cool and put together. She was very specific.

"Socially, it is the most important thing you can do," she had said.

Veronica had rolled that pearl of wisdom around her mind all summer. With proper tailoring, cool and put together were just within reach. In fact they were only seven inches away. But children are not the captains of their own ships. Grown-ups are. The tailor and her mother were at the helm and they steered Veronica's ship straight into an iceberg. The tailor convinced her mother that since Veronica was still growing it was necessary to leave the newly acquired Randolf uniform nearly as it was. In other words: not cool and not the least bit put together.

Here she was, the first day of her new life, her finger rubbed raw and her future capsized. Her parents said she was being dramatic. Oh really? Was it dramatic to mourn the end of your life? Veronica Louise Morgan thought not. She was the smallest Morgan, sandwiched between two bigger Morgans who always sided against her. People in charge so rarely take responsibility.

At least there was Cadbury. She would see him this afternoon. Cadbury was the puppy that had arrived at Paws and Claws eight weeks ago. His face was the first thing Veronica thought about every morning and the last thing she imagined before she fell asleep at night. All summer she had asked her parents to buy him. They said, "Maybe." But it turns out *maybe* is just a word that makes parents seem less mean before they say "We'll see" and other time-stalling things parents say before they finally say "No" and "The discussion is over." When she had children, Veronica decided, the discussion would never be over.

The idea of Cadbury being sold to people who could never love him as much as Veronica did was a thought worse than death. It was a crime she had to prevent. But first she had to get through her first day at the Randolf School for Girls.

Ugh.

Matryoshka Morgans

Veronica and her parents waited for the elevator in descending-size order. They were a set. But Veronica didn't feel she belonged. She needed someone who would see her point of view, a sister. Everyone said having a sibling wasn't all it was cracked up to be. Take Poppy Greenblatt. She'd been left alone with her little brother Walter for all of five minutes and had accidentally poked his eye out. "Well, of course she did!" Mrs. Morgan had said. "Poor Poppy isn't the center of her parents' lives anymore." Mrs. Morgan always had sympathy for the wrong person in the story. Wasn't Walter Greenblatt the glass-eyed toddler the tragic character?

The elevator arrived and Mr. and Mrs. Morgan ushered their daughter inside. Veronica's stomach was in knots. She experimented with her posture, trying to make her uniform look shorter. Mr. Morgan pushed the button for the lobby while her mother fussed with her hair.

"We have got to get you a haircut," Mrs. Morgan said with a kind of exasperation that Veronica took personally. "Your hair is so long, honey, it just *pulls* your whole face *down*."

Veronica grimaced. A haircut was not the answer. The answer was a shorter uniform.

The elevator deposited the three Morgans in the lobby and there was Charlie, Veronica's favorite doorman. "Looking good," he said. "Today's the big day!" He smiled and cocked his cap. She loved when he did that. It was like their secret handshake.

"Charlie! You are so sweet!" said Mrs. Morgan. Why was her mother answering people who weren't talking to her? Obviously Charlie was addressing *Veronica* Morgan, not *Marion* Morgan. Veronica's finger wormed its way inside a pleat and she gave it a good rub. That was one small virtue about wearing a uniform, she supposed. She could probably rub her finger till it bled and no one would even know.

Outside the September air hung heavy and humid. At the corner of Ninety-Eighth Street and Fifth Avenue Marvin Morgan said, "Hey, I'm noticing something!" Veronica exchanged a look with her mother. "You two are always mad at me for not noticing anything. Well, I'm noticing something."

It was true. Veronica's father rarely noticed anything.

Last year her mother had experimented with dyeing her hair red and it took him three days to comment, and even then he got the color wrong.

"What are you noticing, Marvin?" asked his wife.

"Straight ahead. Isn't that the same whatchamajig Veronica is wearing?" Veronica and her mother looked, and up ahead, another girl was wearing a Randolf uniform.

"Marvin! Very good noticing."

"There's another one," he said proudly. He pointed to a girl with wavy hair the color of honey. Her uniform was at least as long as Veronica's. She wasn't the kind of person Lynn Dehavenon would have considered cool and put together.

"Let's catch up with her," Mrs. Morgan said, beginning to run. "Maybe she's in your class."

"Mother, please!" said Veronica. But Mrs. Morgan was already halfway down the block.

"How many times do I have to tell her I'm shy?" Veronica asked her father. He knew her predicament better than anyone, but he never stood up for her. Just once Veronica would appreciate her parents taking her side instead of simply reminding her that she was loved. A sister would take her side.

When Mr. Morgan and Veronica caught up with Mrs. Morgan they found her merrily interrogating the honey-haired girl.

"—and how long have you attended Randolf? We think it is the most lovely school!" Which was more awful? Veronica wondered. Your mother trying to make friends for you or a total stranger seeing how crazy your family was? Veronica counted on empathy from the girl but instead all she got was a look entirely void of emotion. Veronica was crushed.

"Veronica," Mrs. Morgan said, "this is Sylvie. She not only goes to Randolf, as we can tell by her stunning uniform, she's in your class!"

"Pretty crazy," Sylvie said.

"Yessir," Veronica said. It was obvious they were never going to be friends.

She tried not to worry, not because she had a shred of confidence about her future, but because when she was worried she looked worried and when she looked worried it had a bad effect on people. And she still had a whole school's worth of people to meet.

At the corner of Ninety-First and Madison her parents asked if she wanted them to come inside with her. They were in front of the little bakery where Mrs. Morgan and Veronica sometimes indulged in chocolate croissants.

"I cleared the whole morning," Mrs. Morgan said.

"We could at least walk you in," her father suggested. He gave his daughter's hand a little squeeze. Were they kidding? If Sylvie didn't think badly of her before, she had to now. Sylvie wasn't even walking with one of her parents, let alone both of them. Veronica let go of her father's hand.

"No, thanks," she said.

"Have a great day! I love you, honey," Mrs. Morgan said. She reached over for a hug, awkwardly smashing her purse into the side of Veronica's backpack.

"Goodbye, Sylvia," her father said. "Love you, Veronica."

"Sylvie, not Sylvia. I love you too," Veronica mumbled. Ugh.

Her parents left together, and Veronica tried to get her bearings. Two girls running toward each other caught her eye. It couldn't be, but they looked like they were running in slow motion. They were a mirror image of each other in their uniforms and matching bright pink cashmere cardigans. Their cheeks were flushed and their hair gleamed.

"Athena Mindendorfer! I love what you're wearing!"

"Sarah-Lisa Carver! I love what *you're* wearing. You must be some kind of a style genius to pair that uniform with that cardigan." They hugged madly.

They were definitely the kind of girls Lynn Dehavenon would consider cool and put together, but what Veronica envied most was their friendship.

In all the years of being best friends with Cricket Cohen, she'd worried constantly about liking Cricket

Cohen more than Cricket Cohen liked her. Whenever she'd brought it up, Cricket always said, "Veronica, you never think people like you." At which point Cricket would walk away leaving Veronica with the distinct sensation that nobody liked her.

The cardigan twins entered the school in a synchronized, practically choreographed manner. Aside from coveting their friendship, Veronica wanted their tailor. Their uniforms were perfect.

Veronica's eye traveled from her own long and baggy skirt to Sylvie's. The two of them resembled a couple of wrinkly furred shar-peis. Those Chinese dogs that look like they will never grow into their own skin.

Morning Verse

Inside Randolf, plaid-clad girls swirled. They ran every which way, hugging, squealing, nearly knocking Veronica over in their excitement. Veronica knew she would feel out of place. But the happy clamor of reuniting friends was worse than she had imagined. Meanwhile Sylvie had disappeared, as though she had better things to do than be attached to Veronica Louise Morgan. Veronica was surrounded by people who must have known she was new. But none of them showed any interest in anything about her. Why would they? Everyone knew new kids had to pay their dues.

Everyone, that is, except Marion and Marvin Morgan. All summer they had told their nervous daughter that the whole of Randolf would be excited to meet her. The stupidity of people over thirty was frightening. Apparently intelligence was removed when you got older. There could be no other explanation. All Veronica could hope for was that when it happened to her, it wouldn't hurt. She rubbed her finger against her skirt, trying to remember why she had wanted to change schools in the first place. What a mistake.

Veronica's old school had a mission, which was to prepare its students for the statewide proficiency tests. Randolf's mission was very different. It wanted to build a student's reverence for the world she lived in through an appreciation of spirit, science, and art. Randolf believed humanity existed inside the soul and outside in the world. Mrs. Morgan thought that this was wonderful. Mr. Morgan didn't know what they were talking about. And Veronica stood somewhere in the middle.

The school occupied an old mansion designed by the same man who designed Grand Central Terminal. Veronica looked at the vaulted ceiling. She half expected to find the answers to all of life's questions etched there like stars in the heavens. Wouldn't that be nice? She felt a kind of reverence looking up at the gorgeous ceiling, so maybe the school's philosophy was already taking root.

A bell rang and everyone headed up the long and gently curved staircase. Veronica let herself get swept along with the crowd. The stairs were made of marble and Veronica couldn't help imagining girls floating up and down, wearing ball gowns instead of school uniforms. She spotted Sylvie up ahead and tried to keep her in focus. She would know where the sixth-grade classroom was and Veronica was in no condition to ask anyone anything. Not that she would have been able to get anyone's attention anyway. A clutch of girls chattered behind her. They were so close she could almost feel their breath on her neck.

"Are you going to Sarah-Lisa's party on Friday night?" one girl said.

"Of course!" said another. Veronica wanted to turn around and see who was talking. But she didn't dare. There were already parties she wasn't invited to. Just like her parents had said. Everyone was dying to meet her.

The walls of her new classroom were the color of egg yolk and three big windows let in lots of thick bright sunlight. Her old classroom was a pale green. She realized now, in retrospect, that the green made everyone look slightly sick. *Yellow is a much happier color*, Veronica decided. She could see the tops of the trees through the windows. Being in her new classroom felt a bit like being inside a tree house.

Her teacher, Ms. Padgett, stood in front of the class and the way the sun reflected off her blond hair made her look like she had a halo.

"Veronica?" she asked warmly. "Please, come and join us." Her voice sounded like wind chimes. Ms. Padgett walked Veronica to a chair next to Sylvie, who was sitting at a table for four. But unlike the shared tables at Veronica's old school, this one was round. Neither she nor Sylvie seemed happy to be reunited.

"Girls," Ms. Padgett said, addressing the class. "Let's welcome Veronica. Try to remember what you felt like your first day and be kind." Veronica really wished Ms. Padgett hadn't just said that because now every pair of eyes in the room was looking at her and her ill-fitting uniform. The cardigan twins took seats at the same table where she and Sylvie sat. Veronica observed that their hair, though different colors, was cut to match.

"Veronica," Ms. Padgett continued, "this is Athena, Sarah-Lisa, and this is Sylvie. Girls, this is Veronica."

Athena and Sarah-Lisa flashed white, straight-toothed smiles and Sylvie barely moved her head as she said, "Yes, we met."

"Veronica," Ms. Padgett said, "follow along as best you can and in a few days you will feel like you have been with us forever. Right in front of you, please look at your copy of Morning Verse."

All at once, the class rose.

In unison the girls recited:

I look upon the universe so tall,
The sun warms my heart and the moon guides
my soul.

The stars above sparkle and the earth below
informs my feet.

The beast and the pebble, the rain and the dawn,
Side by side.
Harmony to all things, great and small.

Veronica didn't say the words out loud. She wasn't even sure she understood them, but they transported her nevertheless to a world of magic and kindness where dragonflies floated beside colorful butterflies, rocks offered sage advice, and fluffy-tailed squirrels helped mice crack open acorns. It was a world of complete acceptance.

It was her favorite moment of the day.

Cadbury

At three o'clock the doors to Randolf opened, spilling girls happy to be finished with their school day out onto the pavement. Veronica stood in their midst waiting for her eyes to adjust to the bright afternoon sun. She had survived her first day. Now she could visit Cadbury, the lemon beagle at Paws and Claws.

The sidewalk was slow to come into focus. The sparkles in the cement played tricks with her eyes as she followed them east. She crossed Madison Avenue, ignoring the shoe store her mother loved and the smoothie place she loved. There was no time for pizza. She could have a snack when she got home later. Cadbury was the first order of business.

At the corner of Lexington, Veronica saw the orange awning with its three white paw prints. A smile pushed its way across her face. She peered through the window looking for Simon. Simon was usually out in the afternoon, which made it her favorite time to visit Cadbury. Simon owned Paws and Claws. This made no sense since Simon didn't like animals. Simon didn't seem to like much of anything at all, except for making money. He tolerated Veronica when she was with her mother, sometimes he was even nice to her, but when she was alone he had no patience.

A cute Yorkshire terrier displayed in the front window jumped up on his hind legs to look at Veronica. Half his body disappeared into the mounds of shredded paper. He was so cute. Veronica wished she could buy every dog in the place. The good news was she didn't see Simon. The bad news was she didn't see Cadbury either. Her heart banged nervously inside her chest like a drum.

If Cadbury was gone she didn't know what she would do.

Ray lurked in the background while Esme motioned wildly at Veronica to come inside. Esme was nineteen. She had jet-black hair with purple and blue streaks and a nose ring and a gold stud in her tongue. She had a haircut that featured long parts in the front and short parts in the back. She wore safety pins as earrings and black lipstick and lots of black eye makeup. Veronica's mother thought Esme was trying to punish her mother.

"Why else would she try so hard to make herself unattractive?" Veronica's own mother had said. But the more weird things Esme did to herself, the more beautiful Esme became. Veronica thought you could shave Esme's head and cover her with bandages and bruises and a garbage bag and she would still be the prettiest person in the room. Veronica adored Esme. And since Esme had graduated from Randolf, Randolf must be a worthwhile place.

Veronica opened the door, scanning the store for Cadbury. Esme pointed toward the wall of cages in the back—there he was. Relieved, Veronica made her way to him, filling her lungs with the damp and earthy smells of animals and kitty litter and cedar shavings and pet foods. It was probably a smell some people didn't like, but it was a smell Veronica couldn't get enough of. It was outdoorsy, but outdoorsy in the perfect way for a city kid because it was indoors. Plus the smell of Paws and Claws reminded her of when she was little. Her mother took her there every day until she went back to work full-time when Veronica started kindergarten. Sometimes they stayed for hours. Her psychiatrist parents joked that they were going to publish a paper about a little girl who was socialized in a pet store by small animals instead of at preschool by small children.

"We could all be famous," her father had said.

"Hi, Veronica Louise. Did your incarceration at the Randolf Penitentiary for Girls start yet?" Esme asked. Veronica curtsied in her uniform and Esme admired her from head to toe.

"Why you bother talking to that girl? That girl don't

never talk," Ray said. Ray ruined everything. Without Ray, Veronica imagined, she would have long and wonderful conversations with Esme.

"Maybe she prefers higher life forms than you, Ray," Esme said. "I know I do." Veronica laughed.

"Snap," Ray said. He shook his head, muttered something in Spanish, and went back to cleaning a hamster cage. Veronica loved the way they bickered. They bickered like family.

"Cadbury has hot spots again," Esme said. "They're healing well, but we had to move him."

Veronica figured as much since Cadbury sat alone in a cage with a plastic cone around his neck and two bright red, oozing patches of skin that had been licked clean of fur gleaming on his right flank. He was desperate to get at the itchy spots. But if he kept licking he would spread the infection. He looked so frustrated. Veronica couldn't stand it.

"Is it okay if I sit here?" Veronica said, pulling over a giant bag of bedding.

"Of course," Esme said. "You can take him out and play with him." Veronica gently took Cadbury on her lap, wondering if Esme had any idea how much she loved her.

There was lots to admire about Esme. She was so completely herself, for one thing. She was confident and opinionated and passionate. That was her way with people. With animals she was a little bit more respectful.

With animals, she always made eye contact and asked permission before touching them, before picking them up, before petting them, before clipping their nails. Esme was going to be an animal rights activist when she grew up but until then she interned at a veterinarian's office twenty hours a week. Veronica had no idea what she wanted to be when she grew up, but she wouldn't mind being a lot like Esme.

Cadbury tried to lick Veronica but his cone got in the way. Veronica stuck her face right inside.

"Poor you. Poor, poor you," she said. She was aching to take him home. For some unknown reason, Cadbury hadn't been sold. All of his brothers and sisters had been taken home within three days of arriving, but no one except for Veronica had wanted Cadbury. Esme had a theory. Esme said no one wanted Cadbury because he was a lemon beagle. All of his spots were pale caramel, except for one brown triangle under his right front leg. He was named after a Cadbury bar.

"Lemon beagles used to be considered a mutation of the breed," Esme said when the last of his litter had been sold. "But really, they're so sweet. And some people say they're calmer than the traditional black, white, and brown ones. Personality aside, they used to be put down because they weren't desirable looks-wise, which is totally fascist but that's another story. Anyway, that's why I hate breeders.

Correction: that is *one* of the reasons I hate breeders. What if my parents were like that? Oh, this child has hair we don't care for. Put her down!"

Veronica agreed it was heinous, but she was also glad Cadbury wasn't desired as much as his brothers and sisters. It meant he was still in her life. But for how long? If only her parents would buy him. He was getting big and this was no life for him. Her parents had bought her pets before, but the leap to dog was too far. It was incredible how many excuses they had for not buying a dog.

Her first pet from Paws and Claws was a fish named Shrimp. Shrimp died when Veronica accidentally overfed him. Poor Shrimp. Her parents bought turtles after that. But they always crawled out of their plastic habitat and that year—the Year of the Turtles, as her family had come to call it—was extremely stressful. Veronica spent most of the Year of the Turtles on her hands and knees searching frantically for escaped turtles. They blended in very well with her green carpet. She had been afraid they would die before she found them. Her parents spent most of the Year of the Turtles afraid of salmonella.

Eventually, Veronica's kindergarten class got the turtles as a gift. They lived in a tank with a secure lid and a giant container of hand sanitizer nearby. Everyone was happier. After the turtles, Veronica pushed for a guinea pig. "I want a pet who is soft. Whose heartbeat you can feel," she had told her parents. But her mother said she could not and would not ever willingly share her home with a rodent. So a dog was clearly the perfect new Morgan pet, right? And not just any dog, but Cadbury the dog. It was so obvious. But her parents didn't get it. They didn't see how time was of the essence, how every day was an opportunity for someone else's family to scoop up Cadbury.

Her parents were preoccupied with non-Cadbury responsibilities. Her father was writing a paper about the correlation of emotions on the skin for one thing and that had totally hogged the attention of both Marvin and Marion, since Marvin read every draft to his wife. His theory was that emotions manifested themselves on the skin.

Veronica might as well be the lab rat for that idea. She was the victim of a finger rash, which flared up whenever she was upset. But the paper wasn't about Veronica even if the theory was. Marvin Morgan would never put his family in any of his papers, so instead he had chosen his patient Edith Kreller, a name he made up to protect her identity. Edith Kreller suffered from psoriasis and an unhappy marriage. Mrs. Kreller's emotions—her stupid psoriasis and her unhappy marriage—were all Veronica's parents talked about lately.

Veronica was so sick of Mrs. Kreller. Why couldn't they talk about Cadbury instead? She stroked him softly, careful to avoid his hot spots. She cooed and fawned and was suddenly struck by a lightning bolt of pure brilliance. In order to convince her parents to buy Cadbury, she had to appeal to them as professionals. They were obsessed with their patients. Cadbury was suffering from all sorts of anxiety and rashes and needed professional help too. He could be their new Mrs. Kreller. This was the answer, she was certain. But would she be able to accomplish this before someone else bought him? That was the question. She'd have to work fast.

"I will get you somehow, some way," she whispered to her future dog. She grabbed her backpack and said a quick goodbye to Esme, who put Cadbury back in his crate.

"See, that girl don't talk," Ray said.

"To you, Ray. She doesn't talk to you. But you don't talk to her either," said Esme.

"Snap," Ray said and helped himself to a dog treat.

Mary

Veronica heard Mary's little TV as she opened the front door. Mary was almost always stationed in front of the miniature TV on the kitchen counter watching some cooking show or a show about celebrity gossip.

"Ah, she lives! Congratulations. You survived," Mary said as Veronica came through the kitchen door. Mary took care of Veronica and their house while her parents worked.

Veronica put her backpack on a stool and her head on Mary's arm. There was nothing quite as soft and solid as Mary.

"See, you are tougher than you think," Mary said, patting Veronica on the head. A plate of sliced bananas and Oreos slid in front of Veronica and before she could ask, a glass of milk appeared. Veronica took an Oreo and dipped it in milk.

"What are you watching, Mary?"

"I am watching how to live forever without cancer by

making a smoothie from tofu and watermelon. You want to try?"

"Okay."

Mary took blueberries and tofu and watermelon from the fridge. Then kale.

"You look worried. They say you cannot taste the kale," she said.

"I'm always worried. You know that, Mary. You don't exactly have to be a mind reader to figure that out, no offense." Veronica unscrewed a second Oreo and put a banana slice in between the two cookie halves.

"None taken," Mary said, and began cutting the watermelon. "How many times we have to tell you. You will make new friends. You'll see. When I came here from Germany, I know no one. Now I know people. Why you don't believe me?" The blender made a screeching noise as chunks of pink and blue and white and dark green churned separately until they were sucked into the wrath of the blades all together.

The pool of ideas the grown-ups in her life had access to was obviously bone-dry since Mary and her mother and her father said the same things all the time. Mary poured thick purple goop into a glass and pushed it toward Veronica.

"And you know what else, Veronica Louise Morgan? Cricket Cohen is not the only girl in New York City. Maybe you make new friends. Better friends," Mary said.

Veronica didn't think she told Mary lots of the things that worried her, like her entire relationship with Cricket Cohen for example, but Mary seemed to know anyway. Everybody knew. Sometimes talking about your problems was no help at all. But try telling that to a pair of psychiatrists.

Veronica hopped off her stool to look for her favorite straw. It was usually in the back of the side drawer where her mother kept various kitchen gadgets and take-out menus though they always ordered from the same Chinese restaurant. She stuck her loopy straw into Mary's latest creation with glee. She had to suck hard at the purple slush to pull it through the loops into her mouth. It wasn't bad, even if it had kale and tofu in it and was probably healthy. Mary was good in the kitchen. All the ladies in Veronica's life were.

"You were thirsty. Now, my baby. Look at the glass. Is it full?"

"Oh, Mary. *Please.* Not the half-full lecture."

"Yah, Veronica. Your whole life, you look at the worst side of everything. I think this year you change. I think good things happen to you at this school. I think you finally will change your perspective." Veronica knew what Mary meant, but she also knew that however she looked at the glass—half-full or half-empty—it was still just half a glass. So who cared.

Mary patted Veronica's hair and poured herself a

smoothie. She drank some and the funny-looking purple mustache it left above her lip made Veronica smile.

"Yuck. You like this tofu business?" Mary said, and spit hers into the sink.

"Yah," Veronica said, "and you could too. If you change your perspective."

Mary laughed. She hugged Veronica close against her soft body and kissed her three quick times in a row like she always did.

Dr. Veronica Morgan, Dog Psychiatrist

On the Internet, later that afternoon, Veronica discovered three things responsible for causing hot spots. The first was tangled or matted hair. That only applied to long-haired dogs, not beagles. The second was allergies. Esme had never mentioned Cadbury having any allergies, so Veronica didn't think that was relevant. The third was boredom, stress, or loneliness. Bingo.

"Your dog," the site said, "may need more exercise, playtime, or attention. Lack of any or all of these things may result in a dog who maims himself by constant licking and scratching."

The thought of Cadbury maiming himself made her finger itch and her heart break. Obviously if Cadbury belonged to the Morgan family, he wouldn't be lonely, so he wouldn't need to hurt himself. Adopting him was good for Veronica and crucial for Cadbury. Why should Mrs. Kreller be the only one to benefit from psychiatric intervention?

Veronica would lay it on thick tonight, at dinner, but she had to finesse it just right. Her parents had to think adopting Cadbury was their idea. Her plan was so brilliant she could barely stand it.

Meanwhile, it was time to walk Fitzy.

"Be careful, my baby," Mary said. "And don't bring him in here to say hello. He is one dog that ruins the whole bunch."

"Of apples?"

"Yah, Fitzy is more bad apple than one bad apple."

"Mary."

"Yah?"

"Never mind," Veronica said. Sometimes explaining the English language to Mary was a lot more trouble than it was worth. She grabbed a plastic bag from the kitchen and headed for the elevator.

Fitzy was a miniature dachshund who lived on the tenth floor. Fitzy growled at the doormen, bit her dog walkers, and took special delight in nipping at young children. She wore a monogrammed sweater and a bow at all times. Perhaps Fitzy suffered from too much attention. Mr. and Mrs. Ferguson called Veronica the Dog Whisperer because Fitzy adored Veronica. In fact, when their fifth dog walker quit, they offered to pay Veronica fifteen dollars a week to walk Fitzy. If Veronica had been able to convince her parents that she would be perfectly fine walking a ferocious dachshund, she had to be able to convince them to rescue an anguished beagle with psychosomatic hot spots.

A Chance for Success

Veronica returned from Fitzy's walk with her plan for adopting Cadbury firmly in place. It was important not to engage with either parent too much before dinner. Her best chance for success would be at the table when her parents were relaxed and eating. She hung up her coat and steeled herself before going to the kitchen.

Surprise surprise, her mother had the Hunan Delight menu in one hand and the phone in the other. How many times a week did the Morgans order Chinese food? Too many. Still, Veronica hoped her mother would order the string beans. She turned on the faucet and washed her hands.

"Yes, chicken with yellow leeks," her mother told the phone. "One order of dry sautéed string beans and one order of loofah. Thank you. What? Yes! Dumplings. Thanks for remembering! Life wouldn't be worth living without your pork dumplings. Two orders. Fried." Mrs. Morgan hung up the phone and flung her arms around her daughter. "How was school?"

"Okay," Veronica said, taking a stack of plates and a pile of napkins from the counter.

"Let's eat in the dining room tonight, okay, lovey? Tell me everything."

"There's not much to tell. My uniform is too long, but you already know that," Veronica said, very pleased with herself. Her plan had three parts and thanks to that last remark, part one was officially in motion. Part one depended on making her parents feel bad about how awful school was, that she had no friends, etc. Part two was establishing how sad Cadbury was: hot spots, unwanted, etc. Part three: BUY CADBURY. She was a genius. Cadbury was almost hers.

"That's it?" her mother said. "That was your whole Randolf experience?"

"Pretty much," Veronica said, putting plates and napkins on the table. Of course she could tell them about her teacher, about Morning Verse, about the two movie star girls with matching sweaters, but not now. Right now she had to stick to the plan. Mr. Morgan appeared from the powder room with wet hands. He kissed Veronica and dried his hands on the back of her sweatshirt at the same time.

"Gross, Daddy," Veronica said. He responded with another kiss.

"What's for dinner?" he asked.

"Chinese," Veronica and her mother answered in unison.

"Oh, yummy," her father said, clearly disappointed. Veronica and her father walked to the kitchen.

"Marion, you're such a good cook. Can't you cook for us? Sometimes? Please?"

"I am a good cook. But I don't know how to cook *quickly*. I have a full-time practice, Marvin." She handed her husband a water pitcher.

"Couldn't you just cook fewer things?" he asked. "I mean, I'm not a cook myself, but it seems to me that if you made fewer dishes, it would perhaps take less time?" He stood at the sink, running water, waiting for the pitcher to fill.

It was taking forever to sit down.

"I don't know how to make fewer dishes. Even though I am in the mental health business, I have no sense of moderation."

"That's for sure," Veronica piped in. She grabbed three glasses from the shelf and filled them with ice. Her mother could hardly be accused of not knowing herself. When she cooked, she kind of went crazy. She made dessert from scratch, she made stocks and sauces and everything was delicious and it really did take her three days to feed the three of them and then she seemed both proud and miserable watching it all get eaten in a matter of minutes.

"How was school, honey?" her father asked. Veronica took the glasses to the table.

"Good luck getting anything out of her," her mother said, patting her daughter's hair as she walked by.

"Fine. My uniform is too long. My teacher is nice. The kids don't care I'm alive."

"Fine is good!" her father said.

"*No*, Daddy," Veronica said. "Fine is not good. Fine is fine. Which is much less than good." The buzzer rang and the night doorman announced the deliveryman. Praise Hunan Delight. They would all be sitting down to eat any minute.

As always, Mr. Morgan took care of the transaction with the deliveryman at the door to their apartment, toting several shopping bags to the dinner table.

"Did you get any work done today, Marvin?" his wife asked. "You've got to write your conclusion. How is Mrs. Kreller? Did you take my notes?" She unpacked the Chinese food containers and helped herself to chicken with yellow leeks. Veronica couldn't have asked for them to get to Mrs. Kreller any faster—it was almost too good to be true!

"Well," her father said, sitting at the table, "I did, but honestly Mrs. Kreller is a mercurial woman. I may have to revise. One minute her emotions are the source of her anxiety and the next her psoriasis is the root of everything."

Which came first, the anxiety or the rash? The Morgan

family spent many evenings discussing things like this, like Greek philosophers debating paradox.

"Every time I've gotten her to acknowledge her withholding husband, she changes the subject to the humiliation of her skin condition," her father continued. "It's giving *me* a rash," he said, laughing at his own joke.

Veronica and her mother looked at each other in silent agreement that the joke teller was often funnier than the jokes he told. Marvin Morgan continued, "She is turning out to be a very unreliable patient. Like Cricket Cohen was an unreliable friend."

"Daddy, Cricket was a reliable friend," Veronica said. She was annoyed. Cricket Cohen wasn't part of the plan.

"Oh. I apologize. I was under the impression your friendship caused you distress," Mr. Morgan said while looking at Mrs. Morgan.

Her parents, whose living depended on just how complicated the human psyche was, were so eager for her to label Cricket a good friend or a bad friend. They should know her friendship with Cricket wasn't all good or all bad. She'd known Cricket her whole life and their friendship had always been less than simple.

"It does cause anxiety," Veronica said. Anxiety could totally be part of phase one. She decided to run with it. "But it's not her fault, she just has the kind of family that always does things, so she's really busy," Veronica said. "And then

I can't tell if she's just busy or she doesn't like me." Veronica chewed, carefully reviewing the key parts of her plan.

"What kind of things?"

"You know, like apple picking and going to the opera, traveling. They're just always super busy," Veronica said. "Whereas *I* have the kind of family that never does anything except read and maybe go to the farmers' market." Even though all this talk about Cricket might contribute to her parents feeling bad for her, it was time to rein it in. "Cadbury has hot spots. Again. Please pass the dumplings."

Veronica loved how nonchalantly she'd said that. They would never suspect she was up to something.

"Here, lovey. And have some string beans, would you? They're a little spicier than usual but yummy."

"Do you think Cadbury's embarrassed by his hot spots?" Mr. Morgan said. Mrs. Morgan spooned a pile of vegetables on her daughter's plate.

"No," Veronica said, "but I do think he is *miserable.* And *lonely.* He has to stay by himself in the back until they're better. Plus, I'm sure the *lonelier* he is, the *worse* his condition gets. What do you call that?"

"A vicious cycle," her mother said.

"A downward spiral," her father said.

"Yes!" Veronica was beside herself. "A vicious downward cycle. If only he could be analyzed. He has the equivalent of doggie psoriasis. And he's probably going to develop small-space microphobia." She worked her face into a very sad expression.

"Small-space microphobia?" her mother asked.

"You know: a fear of small spaces."

"That's claustrophobia, honey. Microphobia is a fear of small things."

"Perhaps I should include beagles in my findings when I give my paper. I bet Cadbury would be more reliable than Mrs. Kreller. Maybe I'll take a trip to Paws and Claws. Do you think Esme would let me have a session with him?" Mr. Morgan said.

"You could analyze him whenever you wanted if he lived here."

"That's true," said Mr. Morgan.

"You would make such a difference in his life. He really is troubled."

"Can I have that other dish? I never saw it before," Mr. Morgan said.

"Chicken with yellow leeks. It's delicious," Mrs. Morgan said.

"Wouldn't it be interesting from a professional standpoint to see if he responded to therapy? He is probably the most reliable patient you could ever have," Veronica said.

"This is fabulous. Why haven't we ever ordered this dish?"

"So let's adopt him," Veronica said. Her parents did not seem to be following.

"We have ordered this, Marvin. You just don't remember. And you said the same thing the last time."

Veronica was dumbfounded. Nothing was happening. She'd said, "Let's adopt him."

She'd followed the plan and all her parents were doing was eating their stupid Chinese food. They were supposed to have rushed out the door already, leaving the Chinese food on the table, arriving at Paws and Claws just as the front gate was closing. Esme would open it and then they would rescue Cadbury from another night of sleeping in a cage and bring him home for the rest of his life. That was the plan. It was sound. What was wrong with her parents? They gave money to homeless people, they bought goats and cows for villages in faraway places so the people there could support themselves, but they would not adopt the most helpless living being they knew. They were horrible. Veronica couldn't bear it another moment. She threw herself at their mercy.

"It is cruel! You promised. You said when I was ten I could have a dog. I turned ten last year! You said when I proved myself with Fitzy I could have a dog. I did prove myself with Fitzy! After a month with us I'll bet a million dollars his hot spots would go away."

"Lovey, for the hundredth time," her mother said, "we

aren't home enough for a beagle. They need constant company or else they howl. The co-op board would make our lives a living hell. They practically got the Fergusons thrown out because of Fitzy."

"But you promised when I was ten!"

"We *said*," her mother continued, enunciating each word, "when you were ten we would begin *discussing* getting a dog. We never said we were buying you a dog just because you turned ten. We said *maybe*. Ooh, I just love this chicken!"

"*I'll* be with him," Veronica said. Her parents absolutely said she could have a dog and now they were saying they hadn't said it.

"You're in school all day, honey."

"Mary's here."

"Mary's afraid of dogs so her presence would hardly be a comfort to a dog who likes company. In addition to which, Mary has a bad hip so she can't walk a dog," her father said.

"Not to mention the fact," her mother added, "owning a dog is very different than visiting a dog at a pet store."

"You have to walk a dog every day, you know," her father said.

"I walk Fitzy all the time!"

"Veronica, the excitement will wear off," said her father.

"And it isn't just a question of Cadbury, Veronica. We need the right dog for our family," her mother said.

"Cadbury is the right dog. He is sweet and nervous and he has a rash. I promise, you will never have to walk him, or feed him or do anything for him. Please. He needs us. Please. I am begging you. *Please please please.*" Veronica looked at her parents. They had her heart in their hands. Her pulse quickened and her mind raced to the future. Cadbury Cadbury Cadbury. Bringing Cadbury home. Walking him down her street. Introducing him to Charlie, the doorman. Riding with him in the elevator. Showing him her room. Sleeping with him on her bed every night. His tail that looked like the end had been dipped in white paint wagging every time she walked in the door after school, the little triangle of darker fur below his shoulder, his warm breath all over her face. She was so excited she could burst.

"Veronica," her father said, "your mother is right. It's a big decision. And it's my impression that you are very anxious, understandably, about starting at a new school and about leaving Cricket, a friendship that caused you considerable difficulty over the years. These changes are bound to trigger all sorts of emotions. But the solution is not getting a dog that this family is not in a position to take care of. I am sorry to say the answer is no. This family is not ready for a dog. And when we decide to get a dog, we will get a dog from a shelter. Not a pet store. Millions of dogs are euthanized in shelters every year. It is just the responsible thing to do."

"But—"

"End of discussion."

"The discussion is over," her mother added.

Veronica excused herself from the table, threw her dishes in the sink, and slammed the kitchen door. Or tried to. They had a swinging door that wouldn't slam. It just squeaked while swinging back and forth until it stopped.

The Friendship Pact

Last spring Veronica and Cricket had thought wearing a uniform was cool. Cricket had tried to get her parents to let her apply to Randolf, but they said it wasn't their type of school. The day Veronica got into Randolf she went to Cricket's house and they designed their own school uniforms. Cricket's was red-and-white-striped and Veronica's was a solid lime-green shirt with a navy blue skirt and a pink vest. Then they swore by secret ceremony they would be friends forever. Like everything with Cricket, it began with promise and ended with doubt.

"Can we make it official?" Veronica asked.

"You mean, you don't think it's enough to say that we will be friends forever?"

"I don't know," Veronica said even though she knew it wouldn't be enough, especially with Cricket. But Cricket surprised Veronica by suggesting they make a contract. Cricket dictated. Her father was a lawyer. Veronica wrote in her best script. She took special care with the expressions: *hereby stated*, *such as*, and *in conclusion*. After they signed and dated it, Cricket said, "We have to drink to it now or it isn't official. My parents always have a drink after signing anything." In the kitchen, they created a friendship cocktail. They poured lemonade and orange juice and seltzer into a pitcher and stirred it.

"Mmm," Cricket said, tasting it from the spoon, "but it's missing something."

"Nesquik?" Veronica said.

"No. Gross. Wait, I know. We have to spit into it. Then it will really be official." Cricket stood on a chair and spit into the pitcher. Veronica watched rivulets of saliva slide down Cricket's chin and drop into their concoction. She wasn't looking forward to drinking it. But she didn't say anything because she didn't want to hurt Cricket's feelings or ruin their friendship pact. Cricket climbed down and gestured for Veronica to climb up.

"Are you sure it's okay to stand on the fancy chairs?" Veronica asked.

"Yes. I do it all the time," Cricket said. So Veronica, egged on by Cricket, climbed on the upholstered chair.

Just as Veronica spit into the pitcher of friendship cocktail, Cricket's mother walked into the kitchen.

"*Get your feet off* my dining room chair this instant! Are you spitting? Veronica Morgan, stop that right now!" Then

Mrs. Cohen took the pitcher and poured the friendship cocktail into the kitchen sink.

Cricket should have said, "Mom, it was my idea." Although Veronica was afraid of Mrs. Cohen, so maybe Cricket was too.

Cricket's mother made a big show of cleaning out the entire kitchen sink with bleach as though the whole place was contaminated. When she was finished, she gave them plain apple juice and told them to drink that in the dining room with a coaster. When Veronica got home, she realized they had only made one copy of their friendship contract, and it was at Cricket's house. Veronica had nothing in writing; Cricket had it all.

The A Team

The next morning when Veronica saw Athena Mindendorfer waiting at the front door of Randolf, she assumed Athena was waiting for Sarah-Lisa. But Athena took her by the arm instead. As though they'd been friends their whole life. It was a dream come true, heaven on earth, except for the fact that the only thing Veronica Louise Morgan hated more than her parents being wrong about everything was when they were actually right about something. Could kids at small private schools be excited to have new people around?

Moments later Sarah-Lisa attached herself to Veronica too, and the three of them formed a blockade of sorts as they walked down the halls. Veronica had no idea if this was some kind of prank, but she enjoyed it, however long it lasted. Mary would have been proud.

"Everything happens for a reason, Veronica. You came to Randolf and were placed at our table because you are meant to be the newest member of the A Team," Athena said as she escorted Veronica to French. Veronica had no idea what the A Team was, but if Athena and Sarah-Lisa were members, she wanted in.

"Veronica can be on the A Team?" Sarah-Lisa asked.

"Yes! Isn't that amazing?" Athena beamed. Veronica was desperate to know when her membership began and what she was a member of, but she wasn't going to ruin the moment by asking.

"Darcy, this is Veronica Louise Morgan," Athena said to Darcy, as though they had not met each other yesterday. And how did Athena know her middle name?

"Veronica is our new project," Sarah-Lisa added. Veronica smiled, not convinced she liked being thought of as a project—new friend was more what she had in mind. But she wanted desperately to be part of their world. Everything in there was nicer than it was in hers. This morning she'd added a striped cardigan to her uniform. Her mother told her that stripes clashed with plaid. But obviously that wasn't the point. The point was wearing a cardigan.

"Hi," Darcy said, smiling, "I like your bangs. Where do you get your hair done?"

"Um, the kitchen table," Veronica said.

"Where is that?" Darcy said, not following.

"My mom does it. At the kitchen table—" Veronica tried to clarify, but Athena cut her off.

"It's downtown, Darcy, her mother is a stylist there," Athena said, winking. "Right, Veronica?" Veronica was about to set the record straight even though it was an incredibly fun lie, but Athena pulled her away from Darcy.

"Maybe one day we can all get our hair done there," Sarah-Lisa said. "Right, Veronica?"

"Come, shy one. Must introduce you to more of the girls. Maggie! Maggie! Have you met Veronica?" Athena took Veronica by the hand and raced in the direction of a girl with braids. Sarah-Lisa followed closely behind.

At lunch the other shoe dropped when Athena and Sarah-Lisa disappeared into the bathroom for some important primping. Veronica was on her own. The clanging of all the silverware and the hum of conversation in the cafeteria were terrible. And even though Veronica had been introduced to every girl in her class she hardly felt she could just sit down with any of them. Athena and Sarah-Lisa were her point people.

A shy girl named Melody Jenkins, who was a singer in the children's chorus at the Metropolitan Opera, waved to her. Veronica was grateful, but when she came over she found that Melody was singing softly to herself in Italian and Veronica was unsure how to interpret this behavior.

"I have a solo next month," the girl explained, gesturing for Veronica to sit with her all the same.

Veronica noticed an EpiPen on Melody's tray. She wondered what Melody was allergic to.

"Hey, what is the A Team?" Veronica asked when Melody finally stopped singing.

"The A Team is what Athena and Sarah-Lisa call themselves, because they are popular, of course, and because their first names end in *A*? Oh my gosh. Your name ends in *A*!" Melody said it like the name Veronica took for granted was a treasure chest filled with gold. "Since kindergarten there hasn't been another girl in our class who could join. Except Sylvie."

"But Sylvie doesn't end in *A*," Veronica said.

"Her real name is Sylvia. She changed it in first grade so she could quit the team."

Veronica couldn't imagine wanting to quit the A Team.

"I really think there is a very good chance you will be popular?" Melody continued with her upward inflection. She spoke like Veronica's mother's old college friend from Canada. Everything sounded like a question. "According to the news, people who are popular in life have an easier time?" Melody continued. "I can't be popular, because I am in the children's chorus and my schedule is very demanding? You are so lucky, Veronica. Last year Coco Weitzner changed the spelling of her name to *C-o-c-o-a* so she could join the A Team. But they didn't let her. It's awful if they're mad at you? They aren't very subtle."

"Were they mad when Sylvie changed her name?" Veronica took off her striped cardigan and slid it underneath her legs. If popularity was truly in her future she didn't want to mess it up by trying to copy the popular girls' accessories.

"Um, yes," Melody said.

"So, your mother tells me you were invited on a playdate," Mr. Morgan said that night at dinner. Veronica helped herself to noodles in cold sesame sauce, which she was so sick of.

"Daddy, I am not a baby. It's not a *playdate*."

"Ah. Forgive me. What is it I should call it?"

"I don't know. Going to someone's house."

"A Randolf girl named Athena Mindendorfer invited Veronica over. But Veronica says she isn't going," Mrs. Morgan said, obviously upset.

"That's some name. Athena Whatsnedorfer? You're not going? Why not?"

"Mindendorfer," Veronica said. "I just don't feel comfortable." Which was true. Or at least part of the truth. The other part, which Veronica would never admit, was that she had no intention of acknowledging she was making friends at Randolf and proving her parents right.

"Of course you're going. It won't kill you and you might have fun."

"Oh my gosh," Veronica said, "as long as I don't die, it's okay? What if I almost die?"

"As long as you almost die, but don't actually die, I think it's okay too," her father said. "I agree with your mother. Go to that girl's house. Who's ready for moo shu?"

Veronica's grandmother always said, "You have to eat a peck of dirt before you die." Veronica meant to ask how big a peck was. She wondered if in the end a peck of dirt had been what killed her grandmother. She hated being young enough to be forced into things she didn't want to do. Mary said it was time for open windows. Randolf was supposedly an open window. She hoped when she went through the open window that was Athena she wouldn't fall and hit her head and get a concussion. And die. Ugh.

The Goddess Athena

As they walked home toward the East River, Athena told Veronica she lived in a carriage house.

"I literally live in a hay loft," she said. "My living room is where the horses that belonged to the rich people who owned the real house lived. It wasn't designed for people. So don't expect much."

Veronica had never been to a carriage house or even heard of one before and the way Athena said it made Veronica think there was something she should prepare for. She could hardly wait.

The carriage house was set back from the street, hidden behind another house and covered in ivy. It didn't look like New York City. It was tiny, made of wood, and perfect. Veronica could imagine Mrs. Mindendorfer placing all the objects in her little house with the same care and precision Veronica had taken while setting up her own dollhouse. She hoped Athena had a dollhouse. Veronica adored miniatures.

"Hi, goddesses. I'm in the living room," a man said. Athena rolled her eyes. "How was your day?" the man continued. "Sarah-Lisa, I have that origami paper for you." The man was lying on a beige couch in a haze of smoke. Athena clenched her teeth.

"Sarah-Lisa isn't here, Billy," she said, barely opening her mouth. Veronica didn't get the impression Athena liked Billy much.

"I thought I heard someone come in with you."

"You did, but it isn't Sarah-Lisa." Veronica waited behind Athena, looking around at the open living room. There was a balcony that went around the edges of the room. Veronica tried to imagine the room as it had been when horses lived there. She wondered what the balcony had been used for.

"Come here. Let me meet your friend," Billy said. Veronica tried to identify the strong odor of the smoke. It must have been incense, or a candle.

"That's okay. We have a lot of homework," Athena said, and she took Veronica up the narrow crooked staircase. They didn't go to the kitchen and have a snack, probably because Athena wanted to avoid Billy. Veronica was hungry, but she didn't want to look a gift horse in the mouth, especially in an old stable. After all, she was at Athena Mindendorfer's without Sarah-Lisa.

"Is that your father?" Veronica asked.

"No," Athena said as they walked along the exposed hallway, which had a railing. Veronica would have liked a little more information. She half hoped Mary would come and pick her up early.

Athena was leading them to a cross between a set of stairs and a ladder. The two little rooms on the second floor must have been where they kept feed a long time ago. Or saddles. Or supplies. The house was interesting enough, but what really surprised Veronica was Athena's bedroom. She had never seen a girl's room like Athena's. There were no toys in it. Instead of a normal bed, Athena slept on a daybed against the wall. There were more books in there than Veronica had ever seen in such a small space. Athena must be an avid reader, or else this room had been a library at one time. Dried flowers hanging upside down from black ribbons were all over the place, which Athena said she got at her father's opening nights. He was a theater director.

The main attraction of the room was a swinging rope chair. It was suspended from big hooks screwed into the ceiling. It hung in front of navy blue velvet drapes tied back with colorful tassels. They were definitely not curtains. They were too fancy.

Athena put her bag on a little velvet chair (she called it a slipper chair) and, instead of sitting on the daybed with all the pillows, sat in the rope chair. Veronica figured Athena was relaxing, but it wouldn't relax Veronica to sit on a chair that looked neither safe nor comfortable. Occasionally Athena put her feet on the ground so she could turn herself around and around until the ropes on either side got twisted.

Veronica used to do that on the swings in the park. She and Cricket would twirl the chains of their swings until they were tight and all the way twisted, and on the count of three, they would lift their feet and let the swings unwind in wild abandon. It always made Veronica dizzy.

She climbed up on Athena's bed. She couldn't get over the fact that Athena did not have a single stuffed animal. What had Athena done? Grown out of stuffed animals? How could a person not have a single soft thing from childhood in their room?

"My aunt brought me this from Paris." Athena reached over and handed something round and heavy to Veronica. "Have you been to Paris?" she asked. Veronica examined the glass paperweight in her hand. It had a butterfly suspended inside. The poor butterfly looked like it was trapped and flying.

"No," Veronica said. It figured that Athena went places like Paris.

"My aunt goes for work all the time and she took me. She always travels first class. Have you ever been first class?"

"No," Veronica said, again.

"Oh my God, it is the most amazing thing. They have real glasses and real china and real silver and they bring you hot towels for your face and little dishes of warmed nuts before the plane even takes off. You get a menu and they actually bake cookies on the plane for you!"

Veronica was nervous about Billy falling asleep on the couch downstairs and setting the little wooden house on fire. What if she and Athena died on their first playdate? She would love to see the look on her parents' faces when they discovered the playdate they'd forced upon her had in fact killed her.

"Do you like Randolf?" Athena asked.

"Yes," Veronica said. "Because you guys are so nice. I was never that nice to a new kid."

"I would love to be new. At Randolf, we've known each other for so long. Maybe I will go somewhere else for high school, but I doubt it."

"I don't like changing," Veronica said. In fact, that had been a major selling point about Randolf. She wouldn't have to apply to a new high school after middle school. Athena wound the swing chair tighter. Then she pushed off and turned and turned and turned, really quickly. Veronica tried not to look at the hooks she was sure would come loose from the ceiling.

"What would you want to change?" she asked. Wasn't

being Athena Mindendorfer the greatest thing in the world?

"Almost everything," Athena said. "Anything. Everything. I wish I lived in an ordinary apartment instead of this. Wait till you see Sarah-Lisa's house. That's a nice house. And I'd like to live in another country. When I'm older, I will. I'll be an au pair in France."

Mary showed up at exactly five. Billy never got off the couch, and they saw themselves out. Veronica felt like she had been on a long trip.

"I think is going good! Your new school!" Mary announced.

"What makes you say that?" Veronica asked.

"Open doors, my baby. Open windows."

"Speak English, Mary."

"I am speaking English. Don't make fun of my accent, my baby."

"I'm not making fun of your accent. I am making fun of you," Veronica said, following Mary inside a bodega. They picked up milk and sponges. Veronica eagerly took the bag from the Indian man behind the counter so Mary wouldn't have to carry it. She loved helping Mary and whatever Mary did, even if it was ironing, seemed so appealing.

Athena and Sarah-Lisa were like that too.

Veronica felt years behind girls like Sarah-Lisa and

Athena who were ready for foreign travel. When Athena left for France she'd probably go by ship and all her luggage would match. Veronica wasn't going anywhere. Everything she wanted was at the pet store three measly blocks from her house.

"Open windows. You never heard that? It means *yes.* Not *no.* I think you know exactly what I mean. Walk through where there is an opening."

"Well, I went through the open window at Athena's house and nothing happened."

"We will see, my baby," Mary said. "Sometimes it doesn't matter what really happens, only the way you remember it."

Live from New York, the Esme Weiner Show

Simon was hunched over the register the next afternoon, digging in the cash drawer like a dog after a bone. "Veronica," he said when he looked up, "I'm running a business. Not a petting zoo. When are you going to take that dumb beagle off my hands?" Cadbury was alone again in the back. She wanted to punch Simon in the face for calling Cadbury dumb.

"Simon, don't you have somewhere to be? Like the bank or at a meeting with your accountant or something?" Esme said. She was cradling a labradoodle puppy in her arms. In addition to her usual assortment of safety pins she was also wearing a plastic smock. Some dog must be getting a bath today.

"Snap," Ray said. Ray might wear his pants low like a thug but Veronica thought he was a chicken. He'd never talk back to Simon. He probably didn't even have the guts to talk to Simon in the first place, let alone talk back. Esme, on the other hand, wasn't scared of anything.

"I do have somewhere to be, as a matter of fact," Simon said, surveying the three of them. He held a crisp twenty-dollar bill up to the light, admiring it fondly before putting it in his wallet. "And when I return there better be a lot more money in that drawer. Capiche? You got three hours till closing. I want one more big sale." He grabbed his keys and walked out the door.

Ray glanced at Esme and Veronica thought if he could, he would tell Esme how much he admired her moxie. "You look like a shower cap," he said instead.

"Really? You smell. Like you need a shower," Esme said. Her smock squeaked when she walked and Veronica giggled. "Cadbury's still in the back, Veronica. You can take him out if you want to."

Veronica scooted to the back of the store.

"You know another reason labradoodles are a stupid breed?" Esme called out to anyone who would listen. "Their ears are so woolly they always get ear infections. It is practically cruel to create a dog that is going to be so uncomfortable. Mutts, I tell you. Mutts are where it's at."

"Why you always got to say something about everything? Why can't you just, like, be happy or something?" Ray turned up the radio, getting lost in a song declaring life an endless dance party.

Veronica sat with Cadbury, who tried, enthusiastically, to get some good sniffs of Veronica even though his cone was in the way.

"Ray. Have you learned nothing from me?" Esme asked. "America is falling apart. There is no affordable housing. No middle class. No attention to infrastructure. It is just consume, consume, consume, waste, waste, waste."

Ray gave Esme a look and turned off his radio. He walked toward her and stuck a rubber bone under her mouth like a microphone. "Please join us tomorrow for another hour of *Everything Wrong with the World*, with your host Esme Weiner."

Esme laughed. So did Veronica, even though it seemed like Esme really should have a radio show or some platform somewhere so she could expound on all her favorite topics.

"Seriously," Esme said, "we should be taking care of what already exists instead of just always inventing and buying new things. The earth and its well-being should be the religion we organize around. Don't get me started on honeybees. Do you know that there is a village in China that had to pollinate the trees themselves? It took, like, a whole year." She fussed with the hose and the knobs, feeling the temperature of the water.

"But, Esme," Veronica chimed in, "aren't you kind of saying that since puppy mills are so bad, dogs in pet stores shouldn't be bought? What about Cadbury. You know how much I wish I could buy him."

"Oh, my poor sweet innocent child," Esme said. Veronica waited for the rest of that thought, but Esme turned to the puppy instead. "Here, how is this temperature?"

The labradoodle licked Esme, which Esme seemed to take as an indication that the temperature was good. She sprayed the puppy and managed to pay perfect attention to his shampoo as she went back to addressing Veronica. "Of course, Veronica, this is no life for Cadbury. I am just saying if I were God, there would be no pet stores, no puppy mills. There would only be a way to rescue and foster animals. Okay, my little hypoallergenic friend, you are clean."

A wet labradoodle is not a pretty labradoodle. The little puppy looked ashamed. He shook himself off with a force that was impressive.

Ray got completely soaked.

"Esme! What the—?" he yelled. Veronica and Esme laughed uncontrollably.

"Can you believe some rich lady with a botoxed kneecap is going to come in here and spend over two grand on this dog?" Esme asked.

Five minutes later, a curly-haired family came in and bought a leash, a harness, a fancy leather collar, twenty pounds of dog food, and a hundred dollars' worth of dog toys, and paid $2,570 for the labradoodle.

Could it really be that easy for some people? Veronica pressed her face into Cadbury's cone. His breath was meaty.

"Pretty soon I won't be able to visit as much. I'll start getting homework," she said. Much to her surprise, Cadbury didn't take the news hard. His tail wagged against her lap, making such a racket Veronica had to laugh at the ridiculousness of it all. He was an orphan, unwanted, covered in hot spots, imprisoned by the cone—the list of injustices was endless. But he wagged his tail uncontrollably because he could be happy under almost any circumstance.

"I want to be like you," Veronica told him. "If I were you I'd be so mad at Simon, at living in this way, at a million things. I am mad at a million things." Cadbury came closer and gazed at her from deep inside his cone. "But you don't hold grudges, do you? Your glass is always half-full, isn't it?" she said.

She hated putting him back in his cage when it was time to leave.

"I love you," she said as she gently closed the latch.

Veronica swore she felt his heart beating through the cage. She could definitely feel her own.

Morning Meeting

Friday morning Ms. Padgett led her sixth-grade class down the marble stairs for their first assembly and their first Morning Meeting of the school year. Veronica had heard about the once-weekly Randolf tradition during her interview, but no one had really been able to explain it then and now she still had no idea what to expect because the only thing anyone around her was talking about was Mr. Bower, the new science teacher.

"He's so handsome," Darcy Brown whispered to Athena, who giggled.

"Do you like Mr. Bower?" Athena asked Veronica.

Mr. Bower ate a lot of roughage. Why did girls her age care about boys? Or men? "He reminds me of a hamster," Veronica said.

"Veronica, he looks nothing like a hamster," Sarah-Lisa said. "He is the most handsome man on earth."

"Well, geez, not literally a hamster, but he's always gnawing on a carrot or a piece of celery."

Sarah-Lisa turned red.

Darcy shook her wavy hair as though the thought of Mr. Bower munching on anything made her scalp tingle. "The new girl's funny," she said. She always wore her hair loose even though it had been recommended by every single teacher that she pull it back so she would stop playing with it all day.

"He is very very handsome, I agree, Sarah-Lisa," Athena said. "And I would clean his cage. Or peel his carrots!"

"Gross! Gross! Gross! Double gross!" Selma Wong said.

"*Disgusting!*" Maggie Fogel said, which sent the other girls into bursts of giggles. Maggie Fogel reminded Veronica of the girl on the cover of *Anne of Green Gables*. She'd never read *Anne of Green Gables*, but still. Maybe it was the braids.

"Oh, Maggie, grow up. We're not babies anymore. It's perfectly appropriate to think a man is handsome," Sarah-Lisa said. She smoothed her cardigan and adjusted her hair. "Right, Athena?"

"Right, S-L," Athena concurred. Then she and Sarah-Lisa blushed and simultaneously applied lip gloss. Veronica wondered if they were aware that the green of their cardigans was clashing wildly with the flush in their cheeks. They looked like Italian flags.

"If I were a senior, I would want to marry him," a girl named Becky Shickler piped in. Becky reminded Veronica of Piglet because of how cute and small she was.

"He's like a mountain man, you guys," Coco Weitzner said. She was all legs and limbs and a mouthful of braces.

"Yeah, but a really handsome mountain man," Sarah-Lisa declared.

"Okay, we get the picture, Sarah-Lisa," Maggie said.

"That's for sure!" Darcy said, running her hand through her wavy brown hair.

As they approached the landing, Sylvie piped up. "At least he's not trying to be cool like Mr. Chin was last year." Her bitten nails were painted black. Veronica bit her nails too, but she'd never put color on to attract attention to them. "What a poser-loser."

Sylvie made *poser* rhyme with *loser.* She didn't seem to care if anyone agreed with her or not. Maybe that's why she quit the A Team. The whole point of being on the A Team was matching the other people on the A Team.

"I liked Mr. Chin," Melody Jenkins said. "Didn't you?"

"Oh, Melody. You would," Darcy said.

Torrents of laughter rolled down the stairs. Ms. Padgett turned around and looked at her class. It was almost time for Morning Meeting and they were expected to behave.

Single file, Ms. Padgett's class made their way into the auditorium.

Sunlight burst through the row of little leaded windows that went all along where the high walls met the ceiling. Particles of dust drifted in the white sunlight, almost like snow falling. It was amazing to think the air might be full of other beautiful stuff you couldn't see because it floated around in darkness.

Veronica watched eagerly as each class filed in. She looked into the faces of her fellow Randolf students, trying to guess what kind of people they were—what kind of books they might like, what kind of laughs they might have, what kind of friends they might be.

Sarah-Lisa smiled right at Veronica, inching her way closer and closer. Both Sarah-Lisa and Athena had smiles that warmed up whatever was near. Veronica smiled back, flattered. It was exciting how hard Sarah-Lisa was working to sit next to her. She climbed awkwardly over Saskia and made Becky stand up so she could get by. Then Sarah-Lisa climbed over Veronica too, nearly stepping on her feet.

Duh, Veronica thought, *I was not the destination. Athena was.*

Veronica tried to get comfortable squishing between Melody and Sylvie.

After a few minutes, Mrs. Harrison, the principal, walked onto the stage. She reached behind a red velvet curtain and turned off all the lights. In the blackness she lit the candle she was holding and placed it on a round table in the center of the stage. The orange flame danced in the silent, darkened room. Mrs. Harrison said quite simply, "Do you come to Morning Meeting with heart and mind prepared?"

Veronica waited for someone to answer, but all the other

girls were looking at the floor. The question made her think about her heart and her mind in a way she had never thought about them before. She knew she could make up her mind and she knew sometimes she could not make up her mind. What about her heart? That wasn't something she'd ever thought about other than it being the thing that beat inside her chest. The beating was something her heart did all by itself. She wasn't in control of that. Was Mrs. Harrison saying there was some other aspect of her heart that she could control? What would you want to prepare your heart to do?

She could think of things she'd like to make her mind do. Like not think about her finger when it itched, like not let Cricket hurt her feelings . . . But what could her heart offer aside from keeping her alive?

Melody tapped her, interrupting her swarm of thoughts. She shook Veronica's hand and nudged her to shake hands with the person on the other side. Sylvie in turn shook hands with Coco Weitzner and two by two the whole school shook hands with their neighbors. Morning Meeting was over.

At lunch, Veronica put her tray down next to Melody. Sarah-Lisa arrived at the table, and then Athena. Maybe lunch was something Veronica was getting the hang of, after all.

"There's a candle-lighting party tonight at Sarah-Lisa's," Athena said, sitting down across from Veronica. She opened her packet of plastic-wrapped utensils.

"Really?" Veronica said. Of course there was a party at Sarah-Lisa's! It was the social event she'd heard kids talk about that first day of school.

"Can you come?" Athena said, flashing Veronica one of her warming smiles.

"Are you inviting Veronica?" Melody said. Veronica almost choked on her milk. How could Melody say that?

"Yes, silly. Everyone's invited. You have to come. Promise you'll come?"

"Sure," Veronica said. She tried to sound like being invited was no big deal.

"You don't sound that excited," Sarah-Lisa said. She put her tray down next to Athena. But she didn't sit. "Athena, I kind of have to go to the bathroom. Come with me?"

"I am. I'm really excited," Veronica said, kicking herself. She was beyond excited. But some little voice always told her to act differently than she felt.

"Athena, let's go already," Sarah-Lisa repeated. "I'm gonna pee in my pants."

"See you tonight," Athena said, winking.

Whenever Athena winked like that, singling Veronica out, she got goose bumps.

"It's gonna be so fun," Athena said as Sarah-Lisa steered her out of the cafeteria. They hung tightly to their purses and each other. They were the only girls in the whole grade who used shoulder bags instead of backpacks.

"See," Melody said. "You are going to be really popular."

Half-Full

Veronica ran straight to Paws and Claws after school. She wanted to see Cadbury and she desperately needed to discuss her outfit for the big party with Esme. She was seriously worried that wearing a uniform for several days had weakened her sense of style. This party was very important.

Inside Paws and Claws, Ray was reading a copy of the *New York Post* at the counter, not doing anything resembling work. Typical. But instead of ignoring her as usual, he put his paper down and looked at her funny. Esme was behind him checking inventory.

"Hey, Veronica," he said.

Veronica scanned the cages looking for Cadbury. She didn't see him. Esme turned around. "Veronica," she said, "I came in after my shift at Dr. Harskirey's and he was gone. You know if I had been here I wouldn't have let anyone take him."

Veronica's heart dropped like an elevator whose cables had been cut. It landed hard, shaking every bone in her body. Esme came around from behind the counter and held her. Esme's arms were warm but Veronica was cold. It was like cement had been poured inside of her and had set.

She had no recollection of walking home, but eventually she found herself standing outside her apartment building, confused. Charlie gave her a particularly enthusiastic greeting and for the first time in her life she didn't smile back. She stared at the rows of buttons in the elevator, unable to make sense of them. She had no idea how long she stood helpless before her arm eventually took charge and her finger pushed four.

Mr. and Mrs. Morgan were waiting at the front door. Why were they home so early?

"Honey, you have to call us if you're going to be late! That is a rule. You know that."

Mary should have been yelling at her, but Mary didn't seem to be anywhere.

"Mary had an appointment with the surgeon, they're figuring out whether or not she needs surgery, remember?" her mother said.

"What's wrong? You look terrible. Did something happen?" her father asked.

"Mommy," was all Veronica could manage to say. She fell into her mother's arms and buried her head in the lovely smell of her mother's perfume expecting to be held, as Esme had held her. But her mother shook her instead.

"What is it? Speak to me. Did something happen? You are frightening me. We didn't know what happened to you. Are you hurt?"

Yes, my heart is breaking! Veronica tried to say.

"Someone named Sarah-Lisa called you. You've been invited to a sleepover party tonight. She said you have to call her back. We had no idea where you were."

"I went to visit Cadbury." At the mention of Cadbury's name her throat got tight. She needed Kleenex. The sound of clicking disoriented her. Was Fitzy here? Oh no, was she late to walk Fitzy? If Fitzy had peed on the Persian carpet upstairs, Mrs. Ferguson would be so mad. It was Friday. No, she didn't walk Fitzy till after dinner on Fridays.

"Honey, are you okay?" Mrs. Morgan said.

Veronica couldn't focus and she rubbed her eyes hard because what she saw was impossible. Bounding over, his tail sticking straight up and swinging back and forth like a metronome, was Cadbury.

"Cadbury!" she screamed. Cadbury jumped up and put his front paws on her legs. Her parents had bought him! For her. Cadbury was her dog! It was unbelievable but true. Veronica got down on the floor so she could put her head in his cone. He licked her everywhere that he could reach. He licked her mouth. He licked her hands. He put his tongue all the way inside her nose. The little lemon beagle crawled into her lap as if that was the place he most belonged. She traced the path of white between the pale caramel spots with her finger like a boat on furry river. She planned to memorize each one. His velvety ears were so soft. He panted in his plastic cone, his warm body pressed against her.

Mary liked saying that things are not necessarily as they appear. And the truth was Veronica had never been happier in her life. She had everything she could ever want. And yet her nose was dripping, her chest was heaving, and she was sobbing all over the place.

Cadbury and Fitzy Sitting in a Tree K-I-S-S-I-N-G

While setting the table for a delicious homemade meal, Veronica caught her parents smiling at each other, congratulating themselves on being such wonderful parents and buying Cadbury. They were often impressed with their own parenting, and tonight Veronica actually agreed with them. Tonight they were the best parents in the world.

Veronica's mother placed the last of the serving bowls on the table.

"You really went all out, Marion! What a meal," her father said. "Yummy. I love your Indian food. Let's buy dogs every day. Pass the whosies, please."

"Well, it's a big celebration. You finished your paper and we have a new member of the family," his wife said.

"Here, Daddy," Veronica said, passing her father the naan.

"I'm assuming, by whosies, you are referring to the chutney and the dhal? But here is the raita just in case,"

Mrs. Morgan said, sending a fleet of smaller dishes around the table.

Cadbury was in front of Veronica's chair. She worked her toes up and down, massaging his little spine. He was so warm, and his fur was so nice, and his tail wagged and wagged, gently slapping her ankle.

"Veronica, tell us about this party tonight," her father said.

"Oh! The party," Veronica remembered. "I don't know. It's like the social event of the year, I guess. This girl's father is an artist and everyone makes a lantern or something in his studio and then they walk around with them. Maybe even in the park." Veronica slipped Cadbury a piece of naan under the table.

"Well, that's exciting!" her mother said. "Don't get him used to table scraps. What time does it start?"

"I don't know but I don't want to leave Cadbury. And I have to walk Fitzy."

"Honey, we can walk Fitzy for you. Isn't the party more important?"

"No. I've waited my whole life for Cadbury. Plus Fitzy has to poop," Veronica said.

"I like your priorities!" her father said. "A good bowel movement is no small affair. In fact, Marion, I would rather have a good bowel movement, or any kind of bowel movement actually, than go to the Lycanders' party next week."

"Daddy!" Veronica said.

Were other people's fathers as comfortable as hers was talking about such matters? She doubted it. Cadbury or not, her parents were crazy.

"Marvin, I really don't know what to say," his wife said.

"Veronica, you should go to that party. Cadbury will be fine," her father said.

"I can't leave him."

"But you won't be leaving him alone, we'll be here," her mother said.

"Mom, he needs me. Honestly, those girls have everyone."

"I think you're being silly, but I can see we won't get anywhere with you, so let's talk about Fitzy. If you think there is going to be any trouble," her mother said, "tell us. Cadbury is your responsibility now and Mrs. Ferguson can always get another dog walker. Why don't you at least call that girl and tell her you can't come. Before you walk Fitzy."

"She is the most popular girl in New York City. I'm sure she doesn't care if I RSVP to her party, or even if I go to her party. There will be so many kids there, she won't notice if I am there or not."

"Well, shouldn't you just thank her for inviting you?"

"Marion, don't meddle. Veronica is old enough to know what the right thing to do is."

"Right, Mommy, stop meddling," Veronica said. Although

she did wish the party was another night. It would probably be fun. But how could she leave Cadbury?

While Veronica and Cadbury stood in the vestibule waiting for the elevator she told him all about Fitzy. "Most dogs and children don't like her. I guess nobody likes her. I mean, I like her, but she can make a pretty bad impression."

Cadbury listened. His dark brown eyes were so trusting. Veronica gave him a kiss right on his leathery nose.

Her heart was a big wet mess of love.

Mr. and Mrs. Ferguson were out for the evening, so Veronica let herself in.

Fitzy growled ferociously at Cadbury. She dug her nails so deep into the expensive Persian carpet Veronica thought she might make a hole in it. Fitzy was so dramatic.

"Fitzy, this is my dog, Cadbury." Fitzy made a noise between a whimper and a scream. It was surprisingly powerful and every time she made it, her tiny body lifted several inches off the ground. She looked hilarious, yelping in midair, but poor Cadbury began to howl. Fitzy's eyes were gleaming and Veronica picked her up, hoping to calm her. Something warm traveled across Veronica's arm and soaked through her sleeve.

"Oh God! Fitzy! Did you pee on me?" Veronica put her down and went in the kitchen to wash off. She rummaged around under the kitchen sink looking for plastic bags. The

Fergusons didn't own a pooper-scooper. Esme said rich, childless people owned useless things like pooper-scoopers. But when Veronica had asked how Mrs. Ferguson liked to clean up after Fitzy, Mrs. Ferguson said, "Mr. Ferguson and I pay so very much money in *taxes*, dear." Veronica had not quite followed so finally Mrs. Ferguson said, "We don't clean up after Fitzy. We just leave it."

So Veronica brought her own bags. Almost always. She was so excited about Cadbury she'd forgotten.

When she returned to the living room, she saw Fitzy looking *very* guilty. Nearby, on the expensive Persian rug, Fitzy had left three tiny poops as further statement of her dissatisfaction.

Veronica picked up the poop with toilet paper and flushed it down the toilet in the powder room. Fitzy watched as Veronica washed her hands with lilac-scented soap and dried them on the guest towel.

"Fitzy, don't look at me like that," Veronica said. "You are not that innocent and I swear if you so much as lay a tooth on Cadbury . . ."

Cadbury, meanwhile, padded down the hall. Fitzy barked louder the closer he got. Veronica wondered if Fitzy was afraid of Cadbury's cone. Then, in a flash, both dogs were up on their hind legs wrestling like best friends. Fitzy's legs were so short she could almost stand underneath Cadbury. It was adorable.

When they'd had enough playing, Veronica took them

out. For the first time in Fitzy Ferguson's life, she didn't growl or pull or frighten a single child. Fitzy and Cadbury walked side by side like model dogs. When Veronica dropped Fitzy back at the Fergusons', it was obvious they were sad to say goodbye.

Veronica had the whole weekend with Cadbury before going back to school.

She put his hot spot cream on twice a day and tended to his every need.

He followed her everywhere, looking up at her with his lovely eyes. He was alternately playful or sleepy and cuddly.

The first night, she crawled into bed wondering if he would sleep right next to her as she'd fantasized. She patted a spot on the comforter as her mother often patted the couch when she wanted Veronica to sit next to her and read. But instead of curling up next to her, Cadbury dug his way under the sheet and blanket, disappearing somewhere near her ankles. His cone made a funny shape out of the blanket. He made little yawning sounds and moved up a bit before tucking his head into his knees and pressing his little doughnut body right against her belly.

Veronica stifled a laugh. She didn't want him to move or be self-conscious. She lay next to him, listening to the sound of his breathing. The warmth of his body next to hers was the nicest thing she'd ever known. No wonder grown-ups slept in twos.

Part 2

Repercussions

Veronica walked to school Monday morning a changed person. A whole and complete person. A dog person. She skipped and sang and couldn't wait to get on with the day, because in just six hours she would be walking back home to Cadbury. She was dying to tell everyone, to tell anyone, the news about Cadbury. Without realizing, she walked a block past Randolf and had to turn around. Lord knows what other mistakes she would make today because of being distracted by thoughts of her new friend.

As usual, bunches of girls were clustered outside the front door. The subject today was Sarah-Lisa's party.

"OMG. The sunset. It was the best candle walk ever," Auden Georges said. Auden Georges had an English accent, which made everything she said sound so much more intelligent than anything anyone else said. Veronica inched in a little closer, hoping to share her news.

"You guys, my mom totally freaked about how late we

went to bed and I totally lied to her. I said we went to sleep at one," Darcy Brown said.

"Are you talking about the party?" Becky Shickler said. "It was so fun!"

The party. The party. The party. That was all anyone wanted to talk about. Veronica looked for Melody. Maybe Melody would care about Cadbury. Where was Melody when you needed her?

The front doors opened and the girls started inside. Athena and Veronica found each other and linked arms.

"Where were you?" Athena asked.

"The most amazing thing happened," Veronica said. She squeezed Athena's arm.

"More amazing than a once-in-a-fall equinox?" Sarah-Lisa asked.

Veronica should have known Sarah-Lisa wouldn't be far from Athena for long.

"I got a dog!" Veronica said. The words tumbled out like cartwheels.

Sarah-Lisa took Athena by the other arm, saying, "I have to show you something in my locker."

"Right now?" Athena said. "Can't it wait till we all get upstairs?"

"Not really," Sarah-Lisa said, and pulled Athena away.

Veronica tried to blend into the crowd.

* * *

Ms. Padgett's lips moved during main lesson, but Veronica had no idea what they were saying.

"So who can tell me what citizenship means?" Ms. Padgett said.

"It means being a useful member of your country?" Melody Jenkins called out.

Veronica doodled Cadbury's name surrounded by question marks up and down the margin of her loose-leaf. Saying the right answer mattered more to Melody Jenkins than anything in the world, possibly even more than the children's chorus at the Met. Why Melody Jenkins didn't end up in the emergency room every week with a dislocated shoulder from extreme hand raising was a mystery.

"Melody, let's give other students in class a chance. Veronica? Did you do anything this weekend that displayed good citizenship?"

"Um, I cleaned up my new dog's poop," Veronica said.

"That's why you skipped my party?" Sarah-Lisa said, loud enough for everyone to hear. Everyone laughed, even the teacher.

"Excellent," Ms. Padgett said. "You took care of an animal by giving it exercise and you took care of the city you live in by not littering. You were an excellent citizen indeed! Sarah-Lisa, I am sure your party was spectacular, but let's stay on topic. Shall we? Anyone else?"

"I think I am on topic," Sarah-Lisa said. "I have my

beginning-of-the-year party as a way of building community," she continued. "I was being a good citizen."

Veronica wanted to disappear.

"It's wonderful how inclusive your parties are, Sarah-Lisa. It must feel disappointing when people don't accept your kindness and yet, to embarrass people in front of other people is also unkind," Ms. Padgett said. She smiled at Veronica, who was grateful. "Please bear in mind, though, that everyone moves at their own pace through their own lives," Ms. Padgett continued. "Any other ways people practiced good citizenship?"

"My father was going to throw out some yogurt containers. But I washed them and packed my lunch in them," Sylvie said.

Sylvie reminded Veronica of an old Sasha doll she had loved but then ruined by giving her too many haircuts. Sylvie should really deal with her hair. Or join a motorcycle gang and live in a basement somewhere.

"This is great, you guys," Ms. Padgett said.

Veronica wished she had been the only good citizen in the class. She knew this wasn't very nice and would not make the world a better place, which was sort of the whole idea behind good citizenship. But she had liked it when Ms. Padgett had singled her out.

"I took the bus to lunch with my grandmother instead of driving. My parents always take the driver," Darcy said.

"I see a theme in our class. Does anyone else?"

"Global warming?" said Melody Jenkins.

"Yes, Melody," Ms. Padgett said. Melody's head swiveled around, grinning. "I think many of you share a concern for the environment, which is absolutely wonderful and it means you are going to love this year's curriculum because we are focusing on ways people and progress and society affect the environment."

Funnily enough, Veronica had thought about the very same thing yesterday. She and her mother had been going to buy Cadbury a toy and Fifth Avenue was being attacked by jackhammers. Construction workers were busting up chunks of concrete and Veronica watched spellbound. Under Fifth Avenue was just dirt. Dirt and roots and pebbles and bugs and who knew what else.

"Don't you remember all the pictures of the olden days in the Museum of the City of New York? Most of Manhattan was once farmland. It wasn't always a city," her mother had said. It was so obvious. Cities weren't literally made of concrete. The concrete was on top of the dirt. Thinking of New York City without sidewalks—being a giant patch of weeds and wildflowers—was amazing to the mind of a city girl like Veronica.

"Let's look at the closing lines of that poem by Yeats that I asked you to read this weekend," Ms. Padgett continued. The girls opened their books and Ms. Padgett read aloud:

O chestnut-tree, great-rooted blossomer,
Are you the leaf, the blossom or the bole?
O body swayed to music, O brightening glance,
How can we know the dancer from the dance?

"All right, my ladies, any thoughts?"

When Veronica read the poem over the weekend an image of a tree came clearly into her mind. She wasn't sure she'd ever seen a chestnut tree in real life so she compared her idea against reality by looking on the Internet. The image of the actual chestnut tree was very similar to the one she'd imagined. When her intuition was correct like this it made her think that her own brain was full of everything she would ever need to know if she only knew how to access it. She wanted to express this to Ms. Padgett, but she didn't know how without sounding stupid.

"Okay," Ms. Padgett said, "let's start with the beginning. What do you see in your mind?"

"A giant tree," Becky Shickler said.

"Did anyone else see a giant tree?" Ms. Padgett asked. Almost everyone's hands shot up in the air. Melody was waving hers around like crazy. "Can anyone describe the tree they saw? Veronica, what about you?"

Melody slumped. It must hurt her—physically—not being called on. Veronica couldn't believe she was being called on again. She preferred not to speak in public and Melody Jenkins *lived* to speak in public. It wasn't fair.

"Well," Veronica faltered, "I saw a big wide tree with a lot of shade underneath. Which was weird because I didn't actually know what a chestnut tree looked like but when I looked it up it looked just like I'd imagined it."

"Did anyone else research what a chestnut tree looks like?"

"I wanted to, but I was scared it would be cheating?" Melody Jenkins said. Veronica's cheeks flushed.

"It is never cheating, Melody, to answer questions that are on your mind," Ms. Padgett said. "Let's collaborate as a class by exploring this picture." Ms. Padgett hung a reproduction of a painting by Renoir on the wall. "This is one man's picture of a chestnut tree. Does it match what you saw in the poem?" The painting was of a riverbank and a large tree. Before she could control herself Veronica's arm was in the air. What if she was turning into Melody Jenkins?

"Veronica?" Ms. Padgett asked.

"Well, not to knock Renoir or anything, but if I was going to illustrate the poem, I would pick another picture."

"Why?"

"Because to me the poem is saying there is no end to the tree. The branches, the leaves, the bark, the chestnuts are all the same thing. So when I think of that I think of just one giant tree. Not a landscape. Although I guess that picture could be saying the whole world is connected, which reminds me of Morning Verse. The way it says that the sun and the stars and the beasts and the rocks are all kind of connected inside us." Veronica had never talked so much in front of a class before in her entire life.

"Excellent!" Ms. Padgett said. "You know, girls, most of us have been saying that verse every day for so long, I wonder if any of us give it any thought anymore. It's good that Veronica reminds us." Veronica blushed. Her cup runneth over. Ms. Padgett had complimented her in front of the whole class! But what if the other girls thought she was trying to be the teacher's pet? She'd never be able to keep the proverbial glass full. Mary would be so disappointed.

Poopularity

After French, Veronica overheard Darcy Brown, three lockers down, telling Becky Shickler how shocking it was that Veronica hadn't gone to the party.

"I would *never* not go," Becky said. "Even if I didn't want to. She must have a death wish."

Seriously? How could it be such a big deal if she was or wasn't at a party? Half the kids probably didn't even know her name yet, and if Sarah-Lisa was the kind of person who liked to embarrass people, Veronica was glad she didn't go anyway. No, Melody's prediction of popularity was not in her future.

She put her books in her locker and got her lunch. She dreaded the cafeteria. She obviously wasn't going to sit with the A Team and Melody had left early for opera practice today. Everyone was already in groups or pairs. There was no spot for her unless she sat with Sylvie, who was at a table alone pulling the spine out of a whole fish.

A voice called her. "Athena wants you to sit with us. She wants to hear about your dog." Athena waved from across the cafeteria.

Against all better judgment, Veronica followed Sarah-Lisa to the A Team table. She didn't want to, but she had nowhere else to go.

"Well?" Athena said.

"I got a dog," Veronica said, but the words came out flat, no cartwheels this time.

"So we heard in social studies. You are such a good citizen for cleaning up after your dog," Sarah-Lisa said.

"I love dogs," Becky said. She moved her tray over to make room for Veronica.

"Me too," Darcy said.

"Is your dog a him or a her?" Athena asked.

"A him," Veronica said. She caught herself looking at Sarah-Lisa for permission to continue. "His name is Cadbury," Veronica said finally. "He's a lemon beagle and he weighs twenty-four pounds and he is white with caramel spots, except he has a dark brown triangle under his front right arm-leg and he has the cutest, softest, most velvety ears in the entire hemisphere."

Just thinking about Cadbury made the day so much better. She missed him!

"More," Darcy said.

"Do you have a picture?" Athena asked.

Veronica wanted to throw her arms around her.

She produced a photo from inside her pencil box. It was just on regular paper, not the shiny kind, but still. It was Cadbury.

"He's darling!" Becky said.

"Ohhh!" Athena said. "Look, Sarah-Lisa!"

"The polite thing to do, Veronica, is at least RSVP," Sarah-Lisa said, giving the picture right back. She'd barely even looked. "Didn't your parents teach you anything?"

Blood rushed to Veronica's ears. She was so mad she believed she had the strength to lift the table, which was bolted to the floor, and actually throw it at Sarah-Lisa.

Darcy and Becky looked a little bit embarrassed, but no one said anything.

Sarah-Lisa, meanwhile, was unpacking the most exotic-looking sushi Veronica had ever seen. She even had red chopsticks that were tapered at the ends and a ceramic dish for soy sauce. Athena, on the other hand, was eating school lunch. Why was Athena friends with her?

Coco Weitzner plunked her tray down. "What did I miss?"

"Not much," Sarah-Lisa said. She lifted a scallop with her chopsticks and scowled. "Veronica was talking about her dog."

Veronica's temperature went up ten more degrees. Maybe Sarah-Lisa would get food poisoning and die.

"Oh. Victoria, did you really get a dog on Friday?"

"Yes," Veronica said. "But my name is Veronica."

"Oh sorry. Ooh, I love spicy tuna roll. Can I have one?" Coco said. "What kind of dog?"

Sarah-Lisa held up a piece of spicy tuna roll. "Athena, do you want one?"

"No, I'm good," Athena said, flashing a smile. "Coco can have it."

Sarah-Lisa dropped one piece of spicy tuna roll on Coco's tray. Veronica unscrewed her wide-mouth thermos. Nothing fancy—noodles with butter and tomato sauce—but made just how she liked. She dug in her lunch bag for a fork. Her mother had forgotten to pack one.

"Wow. Is that pasta?" Sarah-Lisa said. Was this another dig? Veronica wondered. "You are so lucky."

"Veronica, do you need a fork?" Athena said. "Sarah-Lisa's cook always packs one. Like you need a fork for sushi."

"Yeah, duh. Here, take mine." Sarah-Lisa handed over her fork.

"Yeah, duh," Veronica said. "Mine always forgets one too." She didn't mention that her cook was her mother.

"Back to your dog," Coco said.

"Yes!" said Becky. "Your dog!"

"A puppy?" Darcy asked.

"Yes," Veronica said. "He's so cute and I wanted him for months and I love him so much."

"Athena, do I have something in my teeth?" Athena inspected her friend's canines before declaring them perfect. Then Athena asked Sarah-Lisa if she had anything between her teeth even though she hadn't eaten anything.

"Yes. Upper left," Sarah-Lisa said. Athena rummaged around in her shoulder bag, which contained more beauty products than Veronica could even identify. She pulled out a compact mirror and a toothpick.

Sylvie meandered by the table, a book propped open on her tray next to a pile of fish bones. "Oh, man," she said, "is that quinoa?"

"According to the lunch menu it is," Athena said, "but it looks like poop on top of throw up. You want it?"

Sylvie said yes and dug in. Apparently her whole fish hadn't satisfied her.

"Oh, by the way," Sylvie said between mouthfuls, "how was your party?"

"My *party* was amazing," Sarah-Lisa said.

"Yeah. I bet," Sylvie said with what Veronica thought might be sarcasm. She thanked Athena for the quinoa, curtsied, and walked away.

"That girl is so weird," Sarah-Lisa said. "What is her problem?"

God and the Cultural Jew

Veronica walked home wondering why there always had to be a Sarah-Lisa Carver or a Cricket Cohen in her life. A person capable of throwing her off balance and making her doubt her own legitimacy. She wanted to feel glorious and confident all the time, like in class when she spoke up and Ms. Padgett praised her.

She told her parents about what a great teacher Ms. Padgett was and about the Randolf traditions of Morning Meeting and Morning Verse. At six o'clock the doorbell rang, the deliveryman was tipped, and Mr. and Mrs. Morgan unpacked dinner while Veronica set the table.

Cadbury was at her heels the entire time. He was clearly the submissive one of the pair, but Veronica knew he wasn't suffering from feelings of doubt or insecurity. She never sent him mixed messages like Cricket or was mean like Sarah-Lisa. She was a better friend. He knew he was loved, she was sure of it.

"I want to get back to this Morning Meeting Verse business," Mr. Morgan said. "Marion, did you know about this? Where's the beef with broccoli?"

"Marvin, we talked about it at the interview with Mrs. Harrison. You were right there, honestly. You are holding the beef."

Veronica helped herself to Buddha's delight and settled her feet on top of Cadbury, who was again conveniently located under her chair.

"Oh right. And I thought it was crap then too," Veronica's father said. He plunked some beef on his plate. "What happened to the separation of church and state?"

"I'm not in church. I'm in school," Veronica said. She looked over at her mother and they both smiled.

"What are they teaching her over there?" her father demanded.

"*She* is right here," her mother said, gesturing.

"I will tell you what they are teaching her, religion disguised as a cockamamy poem," her father said, stabbing a dumpling with his fork.

Veronica had no idea what he was talking about. She recited Morning Verse in her head. The word *God* wasn't in it. "What's the big deal?" she asked. "We're Jewish, aren't we?"

"Yes, we are. We most certainly are. But we don't believe in God," her father said. "We're cultural Jews, we believe in Chinese food and *The New Yorker*."

As far as Veronica was concerned, this explained nothing. "But we celebrate Rosh Hashanah and Passover every year. We sat shiva for Bubby. Are those cultural?"

"Ask your mother," her father said. "And while you're at it, ask her why we have a Christmas tree."

Mrs. Morgan rolled her eyes. It was hard for Veronica to tell how serious tonight's rant was. Sometimes her father just liked to argue.

"Well," her mother said, pausing with a piece of tofu between her chopsticks, "I grew up following certain traditions and performing certain rituals. A shiva is a way of mourning. I thought my mother would have wanted me to honor her that way. Passover is a tradition. Rosh Hashanah is a tradition. I don't really think of them as religious. Passover's a dinner. We do it at home. I love Passover. Don't you?"

"I guess," Veronica said. "But the whole thing is about how God saved the Jews and how God parted the water. God is sort of the main character in the story."

"You're right," her father said. "But it's just a story. And I don't believe it to be anything more. And I like the food at Passover. Can I have the . . . what is that there?"

"Shrimp, Marvin. They are called shrimp."

"Okay, so, you're into being Jewish but not into God, right, Daddy?"

"I'm not into being Jewish. I am Jewish."

"You know, Marvin, my father said there are only two kinds of Jews in the world: the self-hating kind and the anti-Semitic kind."

"I am not anti-Semitic. I just don't like to be told what to do."

"By poetry?" Veronica asked, looking at her mother.

"By meaningless ceremony and ritual," her father said.

"Marvin. What has meaning to other people may not have meaning to you, but that doesn't mean it doesn't mean anything. People have the right to make meaning in their own way."

"Touché," her father said.

Veronica thought the discussion was over. Her mother had won and since she and her mother were on the same team, Veronica had won also. What a relief.

But her father couldn't let it go. He had to have the last word. "Honestly, Marion, your mother is rolling over in her grave."

"My mother rolls over in her grave every time you order moo shu pork, Marvin."

"Well, she's a lot more upset about your Christmas tree," Mr. Morgan said, laughing. Veronica didn't know what to take seriously, so she started laughing too.

Veronica's grandmother had called the ten days between Rosh Hashanah and Yom Kippur the Days of Awe and she had taken them very seriously. She prayed. She repented. She forgave all who had wronged her. She sought forgiveness from those she had wronged. She considered how to be a better person in the upcoming year and she taught Veronica how to cast off her sins in the East River. On Yom Kippur, the Day of Atonement, the adults fasted and the whole family spent the day in temple. This was the day God decided if your name was going to be written into the Book of Life.

After Veronica's grandmother died the ritual changed. Mrs. Morgan still reflected and fasted but she skipped the temple part and Mr. Morgan skipped everything.

The only thing that didn't change was shopping for special High Holiday foods at Zabar's. Three days before Rosh Hashanah, Veronica and her parents walked into the Upper West Side mecca salivating. The cornucopia of treats waiting inside never ceased to thrill.

"I wish we could have brought Cadbury," Veronica said. "How much fun would he have sniffing around Zabar's?"

"He'd be trampled before we made it to the fish counter. Marion, this is insanity. I told you we have to get here earlier. Every year I say let's get here earlier! What's wrong with us?" Every year he complained. Complaining had become part of their tradition.

Veronica sampled a Lebanese fig Zabar's always carried for the holidays.

"How's that fig?" her father asked. Veronica gave her father what was left of hers and took another. She looked up at the number box. It said *Now Serving 83.* In her hand she held a sweaty *139.*

"Lovey, will you take the list and get what's on it while Daddy and I wait on this ridiculous line?" Veronica loved that people might think she was at Zabar's shopping by herself so she happily agreed.

The treasure hunt began: two bottles of olive oil from Sardinia, a bag of the Lebanese figs, cinnamon sticks, orange blossom water, pomegranate molasses, yeast, carrots, and eggs. In spite of her parents, Veronica still wondered about temple. When she'd gone with her grandmother it was all in Hebrew so she hadn't understood a single word. Now that she was at Randolf she likened the experience to Morning Meeting, only longer. An opportunity to think deeply in the company of others.

Veronica put the pomegranate molasses in her cart, excited about all the delicious food they were going to eat. The carrot tzimmes, the lamb tagine, the desserts, everything was sweetened with honey and dried fruits so they'd have a sweet year. And as if that wasn't sweet enough, they also dipped slices of tart, crisp apples in honey. Veronica's mother always went to the farmers' market and got spectacular apples and several kinds of honey. Veronica loved watching the honey drip down the side of the apple.

One year Cricket and her family came for Rosh Hashanah dinner. Marvin proudly sat at the head of the table, explaining how sweet a year they'd all have and how happy he was to share the New Year's meal with his family and friends. He even said a prayer, in Hebrew, over the challah. He was Mr. Super Jew that night.

Everyone dipped apples into the golden honey and Cricket announced that she wanted to be Jewish. The adults at the table looked like they had swallowed something awful. It turned out that Cricket Cohen was Jewish. She just didn't know it.

Sins Upon the Water

Three days later Veronica, her mother, and Cadbury took their lint and their sins to the Central Park reservoir. The sky was cloudless and the surface of the water looked like glass, as though a blue-green mirror had been placed in a beautiful diorama.

Veronica rolled a ball of lint in her fingers. She felt guilty about throwing something into the water and disturbing its perfect surface. The air had the melancholy fragrance of decomposing leaves and the last remnants of summer grass.

"Mommy?" Veronica said.

"Yes, my sweet?"

"Why do I love this so much?"

"I think because it's just so sensible. I'll never understand whole cities, entire countries getting drunk on New Year's Eve and making resolutions, promises they have no intention of keeping. It's wonderful, setting aside this time to really reflect and consider how to be a better person."

The skin around her mother's eyes crinkled in a way Veronica knew she was self-conscious about, but it made her look happy. A few ducks glided serenely across the reservoir. If Veronica tilted her head at the right angle she could see their webbed feet working furiously beneath the surface.

Mrs. Morgan took a breath. "I will try: not to be late, not to hurry, and to be grateful," she said. "Grateful for all the wonderful things I have." She exhaled and let go of her piece of lint. It drifted slowly over the fence, toward the water, and gently touched the surface, barely making a mark. "Did you know," Mrs. Morgan continued, "there are multitudes of studies showing that grateful people are happier? I remember my mother telling me it was Jewish law to be grateful one hundred times a day. And you could be grateful for seemingly mundane things like brushing your hair or drinking a wonderful cup of coffee. Grateful people will put your father and me out of business."

Veronica took a deep breath and bade her lint farewell. It floated in the air across the reflections of trees and apartment buildings and touched down next to a yellow oak leaf. Worrying, seeing the glass half-empty, taking things so personally—letting go of all the things she didn't like about herself was reassuring.

"I guess Daddy doesn't have sins," Veronica said.

"Marvin Morgan is a gigantic sinner, but we all know

perfectly well that if there isn't food involved he isn't repenting," her mother said.

Cadbury shook himself off and Veronica and her mother laughed. "You don't have any sins, Cadbury," Veronica said.

"You're perfect," Mrs. Morgan agreed. Then she said goodbye to her daughter and her daughter's dog and went home to finish preparing the evening feast.

Cadbury and Veronica were going to take advantage of the mild weather. The whole park was a vibrant wonderland of autumn oranges, yellows, and reds. A playland of tunnels and bridges and hills and pathways, perfect for frolicking. Veronica threw sticks and she and Cadbury chased them. When Cadbury ran, his ears flew out like the wings of an airplane.

Veronica, the citiest of all city kids, felt like a fairy-tale nymph. The chipmunks, the squirrels, and the birds—all the little forest creatures were her friends today. The rays of sun, the moss and the ferns, the wooded paths, they all felt like part of her.

She was having such a wonderful time she didn't realize that Cricket Cohen and Heidi Keefe were coming right at her from McGowan's Pass.

"Veronica!" Cricket called. Veronica was out in the open; there was no way to avoid them or to pretend she hadn't heard. She held Cadbury's leash tightly and walked toward them.

"Hi," Veronica said, "what are you guys doing?"

"We just came from the rocks. We were hiding treasures," Heidi said.

How perfect. The rocks were supposed to be their secret workshop. She and Cricket had pretended to be jewelers in that crevice since they were four years old.

"Is that your dog?" Heidi asked.

"Veronica doesn't have a dog," Cricket said. "Is that Fitzy?"

"Actually, this *is* my dog," Veronica said. She enjoyed knowing something about herself that her old friend—who thought she knew everything—did not.

"You got a dog? Oh my gosh!" Cricket squealed.

Her mother arrived, huffing and puffing. She was clearly disturbed to be walking around in the dirt in her heels.

"Cricket, I have been hysterical. Do not take off like that. Hello, Veronica."

"Mommy, Veronica got a dog!"

"Well, I hardly think that is any reason to scream like a maniac. How are you enjoying Rudolf?" Mrs. Cohen asked.

"Randolf, Mom," Cricket said.

"It's good," Veronica answered. Why did parents never know the names of things?

Cadbury licked Cricket's leg. "It tickles!" she cried. She couldn't stop laughing.

"Cricket," Mrs. Cohen said, rummaging through her bag in desperate search for a wipe, "you don't know where that dog's mouth has been."

Cadbury turned to Mrs. Cohen and began licking her leg.

"No!" Mrs. Cohen said. "Stop that, I don't care for you. Stop."

The girls tried to suppress their laughter as Veronica pulled Cadbury away. But he was fixated on Mrs. Cohen and her ankle. Mrs. Cohen announced that she would wait for Cricket and Heidi on the benches and stormed off, her heels puncturing the mud with every step.

Veronica felt bad for Cricket. It was one thing to have a mom who always embarrassed you by generally being far too enthusiastic and emotional about everything. Mrs. Morgan cried at the drop of a hat. But it must be even worse to have a mother who never seemed to enjoy anything, not even her own daughter.

The girls said awkward goodbyes. Cricket and Heidi went east, Veronica and Cadbury went west. Veronica had imagined Cricket replacing her with someone else. And in her imagination it hurt. But today she faced that reality and it wasn't so bad.

When they got home, Bach cantatas filled the apartment. Cadbury ran through the house and into the living room.

He jumped on Veronica's father's lap, knocking the book he was reading to the floor.

"Did you have a nice bowel movement in the park today?" he said, and rubbed Cadbury's belly.

"Come peel carrots with me, lovey," her mother called from the kitchen.

"I will, but I have to do something first," Veronica said, and ran to her room.

Cadbury jumped off the couch and followed.

Veronica kept a collection of clear plastic boxes on a high shelf above her desk. They were many different colors and shapes. The afternoon sunlight spilled through them casting a rainbow on her wall. She'd never known what to do with them until now. She climbed up on her desk and set her hand on the purple one, which happened to be the tallest.

Cadbury gazed up at her. Veronica opened the box and looked back at him through the purple plastic. She took a deep breath and when her lungs were as full as she could make them she exhaled into the box, filling it with her own breath. She snapped the lid back on as fast as she could. She climbed off her desk, sat down, and took out her gel pens. With her best handwriting she wrote:

Happy Air. To be breathed when needed.

Love,
Veronica

She Scotch-taped the label to the box and put the box on her desk.

One day, she thought, *I will fill all the boxes.* It seemed like it might be a happy New Year after all, maybe, even in spite of her own personality.

Part 3

Winners and Losers

After a weekend considering how to improve herself, Veronica woke Monday morning with some ideas about how to improve the rest of the world. The Three-Day Weekend was at the top of her list.

Ever since she got Cadbury, Mondays were awful. How could anyone expect her to leave a new dog at home and go to school? A dog who smelled like warm toast and corn chips. A dog who was so loving. Cadbury was just as excited to see Veronica when she returned from the bathroom as he was when she returned from a whole day at Randolf. Come to think of it, there should be some kind of Puppy Leave for children who got new dogs. Three-day weekends would be a good start.

She might as well also cancel gym. Veronica Louise Morgan stank at gym. Human beings preferred winning to losing and she was too slow, too clumsy, too timid, and ultimately too embarrassed to get in there and steal balls or score goals. She never helped her team win anything.

Plus her Randolf gym shorts came to her knees, and her gym shirt was big enough to fit two more girls inside. She dawdled in the locker room trying to be the last one out.

"How do you undo this thing?" Athena asked, trying to get out of her brand-new bra and into her sports bra. Everyone knew she and Sarah-Lisa had gone bra shopping that weekend.

"God. Haven't you ever seen a bra before?" Sarah-Lisa said to Veronica.

"God. I wasn't even looking," Veronica said, and left the locker room way before she wanted to. Sometimes she hated Sarah-Lisa.

In the gymnasium, her rubber soles squeaked against the shiny floor. Liv O'Malley stood in the center of the room impatiently holding a volleyball. She was always the first one out of the locker room—she'd probably been standing there for fifteen minutes already. Liv O'Malley was the kind of girl Veronica's mother would describe as awkward when what she really meant was unattractive. She was at least six inches taller than every other girl in their grade, she bit her nails down to the quick, and she had really bushy eyebrows. Tuesdays, Wednesdays, and Fridays, Liv O'Malley didn't exist. But Mondays and Thursdays, during gym, she was a star. Liv O'Malley was really good at sports.

What was the point of knowing how to play volleyball unless you lived on a beach? But no one in the phys-ed department had bothered to consult her about the curriculum, so Veronica gloomily took her place against the wall. Sarah-Lisa and Athena came in from the locker room holding their shoulder bags and each other's hands. When the coach made the teams, he split them up. Sarah-Lisa and Athena tried to negotiate—all the other teachers let them stay together, it wasn't fair, and on and on—but the coach wasn't biting. He blew his whistle until they gave up. It practically punctured Veronica's eardrum, but she adored him for it.

Sylvie was across the net from Veronica. Their eyes met. Sylvie rolled hers. She was the only girl who wouldn't be afraid to do that. Everyone else was so desperate to be in Sarah-Lisa's good graces. Even Veronica. She had no idea why, but she was.

Liv O'Malley balanced the volleyball in her left hand. Her right foot tapped maniacally against the floorboards. She looked at the coach, eager for his signal to serve the ball. In another life, they would probably be married with lots of athletic and bushy-eyebrowed children.

He gave her the nod and Liv's wrist thwacked leather. Game on. Twenty-four eyes followed the ball as it sailed high over the net. It took two girls to volley it into position before Becky Shickler could pop it back over. Veronica's main objective in gym was to do as little damage as possible to her own team. She watched the ball, praying for it to stay far away from her. It flew toward Athena, who was adjusting her shorts. She didn't notice it until it bounced off her foot.

"Ow!" Athena said. "My bad."

"Rotate!" the coach yelled. His voice echoed through the air.

He tossed the ball right to Veronica, who wasn't prepared, of course, and fumbled it in front of everyone. It was her turn to serve. She tried to ignore the pressure of all those eyes and after lofting the ball in the air, thwacked it with all her might. *Please go over please go over please go over.*

It did! There was a first time for everything. Her teammates cheered and Veronica felt great, like a regular girl, like a popular girl, like a girl who was good at volleyball.

She was still celebrating her newfound athleticism when her beautiful serve came right back at full speed. Veronica knew what she wanted her body to do. She knew what her body was supposed to do. But it wouldn't. She was frozen and about to get pummeled when out of nowhere, Liv O'Malley dove in, like a volleyball superhero, and saved the day.

Athena laughed, grabbed Veronica, and said, "We're such losers!" Athena Mindendorfer could call herself a loser because she wasn't one. She was popular. And nice. Everyone liked her. She even wore a bra.

Veronica wished she knew how to laugh at herself. Maybe not taking herself so seriously would fill up her half-empty glass.

Atonement

On Yom Kippur, while her mother fasted and waited for sundown, her father poked at the smoked fish and ate both sesame bagels. When Veronica's grandmother was alive, sundown was when temple let out. Now it was whenever *The New York Times* said. This year it reported that sundown was at 6:27 p.m.

By three o'clock, Mrs. Morgan was hungry and antsy. She asked what time it was every five minutes. "It's three oh five, Marion," Mr. Morgan said between bites of whitefish salad. Veronica wasn't allowed to fast until she was an adult. Not that she was sure she would fast when she was. She had a mother who did one thing and a father who did something else. It was really hard to say how she was going to turn out, but in the meantime she had the opportunity and the encouragement to think about it. Know thyself—that was basically her parents' mantra. Marion and Marvin Morgan both agreed on that.

Veronica lit a candle in her room and focused on her breathing like they did at Morning Meeting. Oxygen was a relaxant, Mrs. Harrison always said, but getting her breath deep and calm wasn't easy. She closed her eyes and tried to open her heart and mind.

Her mother knocked.

"I'm sorry," she said. "Were you praying?"

Veronica looked at her mother like she was crazy.

"I was wondering if you wanted to come read with me while I try not to think about food."

Veronica and Cadbury spent the rest of the afternoon curled up at her mother's feet on the couch, perfectly content. She pondered her mother's question. Maybe she was praying, although until her mother asked, she wouldn't have thought of it that way.

Nothing to Wear

Skeletons hung from doors, pumpkins lined the stoops and windows of every brownstone, fake spiderwebs clung to gates, and Fifth Avenue between Ninety-Sixth Street and 103rd Street was plastered with flyers for the Toddler Parade that took place every year the night before Halloween. Veronica didn't want to be reminded. Halloween was nine days away, and she had no inspiration this year for a costume. And to make matters worse, she didn't know if she had anyone to trick-or-treat with.

She came home from school, hugged Mary, cuddled Cadbury, and changed into jeans. She tossed her white blouse in the hamper and hung her Randolf skirt next to the other six in her closet. It wasn't dirty. She could wear it again. Last summer, these same uniforms had terrified her. They swung from their hangers and made Veronica think of dead bodies. Now they were harmless. Time certainly changed things.

She took her keys, four plastic bags, and Cadbury up to

the tenth floor. When the elevator opened Veronica could hear Fitzy's cries of excitement. She unlocked the Fergusons' door and Cadbury jumped up and down. Fitzy ran a circle around Cadbury and rolled over on her back. Dogs expressed delight without a trace of self-consciousness.

"You two love each other so much," Veronica said. "I wish I could just get you married already." Fitzy's dark brown eyes looked up in agreement. Veronica imagined them in miniature wedding attire. *Great*, Veronica thought, *I can come up with Halloween costumes for dogs but I still have nothing to wear.* She clipped Fitzy's leash to her rhinestone collar and took the loving couple downstairs. Two handymen were arranging a cornucopia of gourds and witches' brooms on the table in front of the elevator. They smiled at Veronica.

"Almost time for Halloween!" one of them said. Oh brother. You couldn't hide from your troubles if your life depended on it. Veronica tried to smile.

Fitzy and Cadbury made a beeline for a tree. But they rarely took care of business right away. First they squatted, stood up, and paced back and forth before deciding where exactly, on a one-foot-by-one-foot patch of dirt, they were going to leave their mark. This was a ritual they had to perform. Why did they do that? There was obviously a lot she didn't know about being a dog.

When the dogs did actually poop, Veronica realized that she had forgotten the poop bags at the Fergusons'. She hunted near the benches, frantic for something to clean up with. A nice lady gave her the business section of her newspaper to use.

"It's very impressive," she told Veronica, "the way you clean up after them. Good for you." Veronica's mood lifted a little in spite of herself.

She let the dogs lead her around while they sniffed the trunks of trees, identifying other dogs' scents and lord knows what else. Cadbury liked to smell trees like this: he followed a scent from the ground up and then back down again, sometimes lingering over a particular spot as if he were sniffing a fine bottle of wine, enjoying a good piece of music, or reading a book and pausing to reread a particularly beautiful sentence. Veronica stood behind him, beaming like a proud mother. He found an old piece of cardboard, which he appreciated like an expensive cut of beef. Cadbury would eat anything if you let him. He'd probably eat all her Halloween candy if she wasn't careful.

She had to admit she loved the candy part of Halloween. But coming up with good costumes, year after year, was too much. *Maybe I'll just dress up as a girl who hates Halloween*, she thought.

"Cadbury, do you think I could just go as a surly eleven-year-old? Fitzy, what if I did that? Would people close the door in my face and not give me any candy because they didn't think I put enough effort into my costume?"

Her companions were not the least bit interested. No

one understood the predicament she was in! Athena had actually mentioned trick-or-treating, but only once, and Veronica was afraid she would forget. Athena and Sarah-Lisa talked about all kinds of things, like Veronica belonging to the A Team, but nothing official ever happened. She was sure it would be the same with Halloween. Melody had talked about trick-or-treating too, but her mother had a million problems with everything.

The dogs pooped again. This time Veronica had to rip down a parade flyer to clean up with. The little drawings of children's costumes reminded her of her first Toddler Halloween Parade. She'd been a cat. Her mother had used a glue gun and even though she'd burned herself repeatedly, Marion Morgan had created a masterpiece out of orange and white feather boas. The costume was so stiff and heavy from the gallons of dried glue that it didn't bend at all. Mary held the neck open and both her parents lowered her in. Veronica could barely walk down Fifth Avenue. But it was the best costume she'd ever had. Her mother had never done anything like it before or since. Veronica hated growing up and being responsible for her own costumes. She'd won first prize that year.

She threw the poopy poster in a garbage can on the corner of 103rd Street. Ugh. Halloween had pretty much gone downhill ever since.

Things Are Really Looking Up

Veronica brought the dogs back from the park thoroughly frustrated by the pressures put upon the human race by organized holidays. Mary was set up in front of the little TV getting ingredients together for dinner. That was a relief since the Morgan family had had Chinese three times this week and it was only Wednesday.

Veronica sighed loudly.

"I thought candy and trick-or-treating were good things," Mary said. "Why the long face? Help me with these beans."

"I have no one to go trick-or-treating with."

"I thought the Athena person asked you."

"She did," Veronica said.

Mary looked at her, clearly exasperated. "Open windows. How many times I have to say that? *Open windows.*"

"Mary, when my glass is full, I will carry it through the first open window I see. Okay?"

"Okay."

"But since I have nothing to wear, my glass is not full. And therefore, I cannot go through any windows," Veronica declared.

"*Mien Gott*, there are nine days till Halloween. We have nothing but time! It is not like you are stuck between a rock and the deep blue sea." Mary could make mincemeat out of the English language while expressing herself perfectly. But Veronica had her heart set on having a miserable Halloween and she wasn't budging.

She snapped her beans and put the little ends in a pile for her mother's bag of vegetable trimmings in the freezer. Mrs. Morgan brought this bag of garbage to the compost stall at the farmers' market on Saturdays. It was so embarrassing.

"Maybe I can be a bucket of compost," Veronica said absently.

"Two months, two months," Mary said just as absently.

"What are you muttering about?" Veronica said.

"Two months I give this hillbilly Hollywood couple," Mary said. She scoffed into her string beans.

"What Hollywood couple? What do you mean?"

"It is crazy the way these people with more money than God pretend to be humble and poor. Ach. I wash my hands. Two months till the divorce."

Veronica looked up at the little white TV. Mary was very attached to shows about celebrities. The bride Mary was upset about today was a blond judge from a reality singing show. Her wedding outfit was cutoff shorts and a ponytail. The groom wore a top hat and no shirt. They were in Las Vegas at a fake chapel getting married by an Elvis Presley impersonator.

Mary slid the bowl of beans closer to Veronica, who took a new handful. "So," Mary continued, "what are your friends going as for Halloween?"

"I don't have any friends," Veronica said.

"What about the Melody person and the Athena person?"

"They aren't real friends."

"Wait. Let me get my little violin and play you a sad song. You know why you have no friends? Cadbury. He is a real-life friend but he is a dog. You should also have real-life friends who are girls, who are at least humans. Melody doesn't seem so terrible. Maybe a little boring, but not the worst person in the world. What is your complaint against the other one?"

"Nothing's wrong with Athena. Except that she doesn't need anyone whose name isn't Sarah-Lisa."

"Look! Again they show that crazy marriage. Look, look, look, they get married like on a shtetl even though they live in Beverly Hills. I bet that Elvis Presley isn't even certified. What is so wrong with a priest? Or a rabbi or a justice of the peace? Nothing is sacred."

When Veronica had imagined Cadbury and Fitzy's

wedding it was very old-fashioned. It would be something Mary would approve of. She looked up from her beans. "Mary, you're a genius! I'm going to marry Fitzy and Cadbury for Halloween," Veronica said. "I'll be the priest."

"Now you're talking, my baby." Mary kissed Veronica on the head three times.

They spent the rest of the afternoon gathering what they could find to make Veronica's costume. Mary pulled an old black shirt from the donation pile.

"You wear this buttoned in the back and we make a white collar?"

"Yes!" Veronica said. They cut a collar out of the cardboard from one of Mr. Morgan's freshly laundered shirts. Mary found an old white mesh sack she used for washing delicates.

"A veil," she said. "For Fitzy!"

Mary claimed to be scared of dogs, but she sure seemed to care a lot about Fitzy's costume and Veronica had caught her cooking chicken livers for Cadbury more than once. In the rag bin under the sink, Veronica found an old black T-shirt.

"Mary, could we turn this into a jacket for Cadbury? Like, we cut it down the middle maybe and put some buttons or something on it to make it fancy?"

"Perfect," Mary said. "Come, let's look in the button box."

Mary's cardboard button box was a wondrous thing. It was long and thin and instead of having flaps for a top, it slid open. Inside were hundreds of buttons of all different sizes, shapes, and colors. Mary had been collecting them her whole life. When Veronica was little they had spent hours playing games with the buttons. The gold ones had always been Veronica's favorite.

Mary sifted through the contents and handed Veronica five very special gold buttons with raised towers embossed on them.

"Here, my baby, will these work?"

Veronica threw her arms around Mary. "Yes!" she said.

Double Booked

Veronica took one of the gold buttons to school the next day because making little outfits for dogs was so fun that she didn't want to stop thinking about it. Plus she could scratch her itchy finger with the raised tower.

While Ms. Padgett demonstrated the magic of cross multiplication, Veronica thought about what color carnation to pin on Cadbury's jacket and the best way to attach Fitzy's veil.

As soon as the bell rang, Athena asked about the button.

"It's for my Halloween costume."

"Ooh, it's pretty!" Athena said. "Is it antique?"

"Probably," Veronica said. "It is from my babysitter's collection." Veronica always felt weird referring to Mary as her babysitter. She was so much more than that.

"Are you making your costume? I was going to ask you if you wanted to make costumes."

"You and me?" Veronica said.

"And Sarah-Lisa, silly. But it seems like you already made yours," Athena said.

"It's not finished yet," Veronica said.

"Oh well, next year. Won't that be fun? We should make superhero costumes with the letter *A* on them. You're coming trick-or-treating with us, right?"

Sarah-Lisa appeared from behind her locker door.

"What are you talking about?" Sarah-Lisa wanted to know. She kicked her locker shut, and Veronica jumped.

"Halloween," Athena said. "The three of us are trick-or-treating together, remember?"

"Oh. Yeah," Sarah-Lisa said. "That'll be fun. Athena, we have to go."

"Slavery is no longer legal," Sylvie announced from a few lockers away. She closed her door for punctuation. "Athena is a free person. You don't own her, you know."

Sylvie headed off to French as if the aftermath of her little speech was of no interest whatsoever.

"What was that?" Sarah-Lisa said. "Wake up on the wrong side of the morning much?" She grabbed Athena and they walked away.

It was true! Sarah-Lisa acted like she owned Athena. If only Veronica and Athena could go trick-or-treating without Sarah-Lisa. If only there was a way to kick Sarah-Lisa off the A Team.

Veronica heard the squashy sound of rubber soles and

knew it was Melody. Her feet always announced her entrance. It was kind of theatrical. Veronica liked it.

"Veronica?" Melody said in her unique melodious manner, turning everything into a question.

"Hi, Melody."

"I checked with my mother, because she is very allergic to animal dander. I think I mentioned that? But she didn't think it would be a problem if I went trick-or-treating with you, as long as I showered afterward. Did you ask your parents?"

Two weeks ago, Melody had asked Veronica if they could trick-or-treat together, but she'd also made it clear that she had rehearsals and that her parents didn't believe in Halloween and that they were allergic to dogs and there were so many other complications that Veronica assumed it wasn't going to happen. But now, it was happening. And she was already going trick-or-treating with the A Team.

"Well, no. I didn't know you definitely wanted to go with me," Veronica said, squeezing the button with all her might. She had barely figured out her costume and now she had to decide who to wear it with. She wished she could go trick-or-treating with just Athena. And if Melody came, that would be okay. That would solve everything. Sarah-Lisa was, as usual, the problem.

The Fourth Veil

Veronica and Mary had great success the first day fitting the dogs in their costumes. The second day was a different story. Fitzy's passion for chewing ruined three veils before Mary and Veronica invented a system. Veronica held Fitzy's nose in the crook of her elbow while Mary attached the veil. But Veronica was nervous that on Halloween, when Fitzy was not muzzled by human hands, she would eat through her veil. Veronica tried not to think about that. Or about Fitzy biting other trick-or-treaters. Or Cadbury eating too much candy. Or who she was going to say no to: Melody or the A Team.

Veronica was gluing little lapels to the black T-shirt she'd found. The next step was sewing the gold buttons in a neat line down the front. Cadbury lay on the floor, panting like the whole experience was too much for him.

"I think he's really getting into the part, poor baby," Mary said. "You know? Maybe the whole idea of being with only one dog for the rest of his life is a little too much. A little too overwhelming. Maybe he wants to stay a bachelor." Mary had never married. Cadbury coughed. "See?" Mary said. "He is allergic to the idea of marriage. Like a lot of men, come to think of it. Now, tell me your pickle."

"It's bad. I said yes to too many people," Veronica said.

"The more yesses the better, no?" Mary asked through a mouthful of pins.

"Oh, Mary." Veronica sighed. "I can't explain. I just can't."

"Two words. Open windows. Open windows."

"Mary, can I say something?"

"Yes, my baby."

"That's four words."

The French Philosopher

Veronica's parents passed the Chinese food containers around at dinner. No one had bothered transferring the food into serving dishes.

"Who do you guys think I should go trick-or-treating with?" Veronica asked them point-blank.

"Well, which party did you get invited to first?" Mr. Morgan said. He unrolled a pancake and filled it with moo shu pork.

"I didn't get invited to any parties, Daddy." Veronica fumed. Was her father not listening? Or was he really unable to follow even the simplest idea?

"You know what he means," her mother said. "Who invited you trick-or-treating first?"

"I don't know. Not technically."

"Technically? It is a pretty simple question," her mother said, glancing at her father. *If only*, Veronica thought. She spread hoisin sauce on her pancake. "Well, Melody invited me a while ago but she had to check with her mother and she only got back to me today and Athena confirmed with me today also—"

Her parents raised their eyebrows, which meant they had just invented a psychological theory about something. Veronica wished they would just be normal.

"Marvin, pass the watercress. Honey, technically, Melody invited you first."

"But you don't understand. I didn't go to Sarah-Lisa's party and I think they're still mad at me about that." Veronica carefully rolled her pancake while her parents watched. They said nothing.

As usual, when Veronica wanted their advice, they kept their mouths shut. Why couldn't they do that the rest of the time—like when she had no interest in their opinions?

Her father was busy trying to remove a fried dumpling from its foil tray with a pair of chopsticks. "You know, there is a very famous story," he said, chopsticks in hand, "of a man who didn't know what to do. His mother was dying in a hospital in France and he was offered the job of his dreams in Germany. 'If I take the job, I will never see my mother again,' he said. 'If I stay and say goodbye to my mother I will never have this professional opportunity again. It is the job I always wanted.' He was paralyzed by indecision. He couldn't move. Much like my problem with this dumpling, coincidentally."

Veronica and her mom couldn't take their eyes off Mr. Morgan struggling with his chopsticks.

"So," Mr. Morgan continued, "the man sought the advice of a famous French philosopher."

"Marvin," Mrs. Morgan said.

"Marion," Mr. Morgan said.

"Use a fork."

"Good idea," he said, spearing the dumpling. "Yummy."

Veronica tried not to watch the pork juice dribbling down his chin, heading for his tie. Mrs. Morgan handed her husband a napkin, which he placed on his lap.

"Your chin," she said, and threw her hands in the air.

"Ah, thank you," Marvin Morgan said, and dabbed his chin. "My story reminds me of Veronica's predicament. Should she go with the one girl? Or should she go with the other girls? Veronica, do you see the connection with the story your wise and wonderful father is telling?"

"Yes, Daddy, duh. The man doesn't know what to do. Neither do I."

"Excellent. So what do you think the man should do?"

"I don't even know what I should do. How do I know what that man should do?" Veronica found herself rubbing her finger on the caning of her dining room chair a little too hard.

"Marvin, tell your daughter what the philosopher said."

"Thank you, Marion. The philosopher said: 'It doesn't matter what you do. Just do something.' "

"That's it?" Veronica and her mother shouted, in unison.

"Daddy! That is totally unsatisfying and completely unhelpful and I still don't know what to do."

"That is because, my dearest daughter, you can't be two places at once, so just keep your word."

"Or, what if you tried to all go together?" Mrs. Morgan said.

"No, Mommy," Veronica said.

What a ridiculous idea. No one told Athena and Sarah-Lisa what to do. They told you.

And yet, the next day, in the cafeteria, that is exactly what she found herself doing.

"My parents will probably like a bigger group," Sarah-Lisa said. "With four of us they'll think it's safer. How many apartments are in your building?"

Veronica couldn't believe it was so easy.

"Well," she said, "fourteen floors and three apartments on each floor—"

"Are there really fourteen floors?" Athena asked. "Or are there actually thirteen floors and they call the thirteenth floor fourteen because they don't want to give anyone bad luck by living on the thirteenth floor?"

"I hate when they do that," Sarah-Lisa said. "Don't the people on the fourteenth floor know they really live on the thirteenth floor?"

Veronica had wondered this before too. Her apartment

building did actually only have thirteen floors but, like Athena said, they called the thirteenth floor fourteen.

"There's only thirteen floors," Veronica said nervously.

"That seems dangerous. On Halloween, I mean. Couldn't we just go in my neighborhood where it is all brownstones?" Melody said. "I am afraid of the number thirteen? And black cats? And spiders?"

"Geez, Melody, Halloween doesn't sound like your holiday," Athena said. "Come on, let's trick-or-treat at Veronica's! We've never been to a real thirteenth floor on Halloween!"

Sarah-Lisa pouted. "But my building has so many more apartments, you guys. There are four wings. There will be so much more candy."

"Yeah," said Melody. "I don't want any bad luck—"

"Please," Athena begged. "We always trick-or-treat at your house. Let's do something new."

The idea that the A Team was coming through an open window, right into Veronica's house, was thrilling. But because Veronica was Veronica, her joy was eclipsed by a scenario more terrifying than thirteen floors, black cats, and spiders combined: her mother acting out while her father told idiotic jokes.

She never should have asked everyone to come over.

Progress

On Halloween, Mrs. Morgan piled Veronica's hair up and slicked it back with pomade and carefully drew two brown lines above her daughter's lip. "God forbid, you look like Hitler," she said before adding dramatic curls to the ends. "Although now you look like a nineteenth-century villain about to tie a young lady to the railroad tracks."

Veronica peeked at the mirror nervously. "No, it's good. I like it!" she said.

She didn't look like herself. She looked like a man. It was a good costume. She picked up the book she had turned into her Holy Bible prop and put it under her arm. Maybe the Bible would protect them from thirteenth-floor bad luck. At least she wouldn't be far from home if and when something unlucky happened.

Melody and Mrs. Jenkins arrived fifteen minutes early, which Mrs. Morgan said was indicative of a form of social anxiety. Fitzy, who also suffered from social anxiety, barked at the door like a crazy dog four times her size. Veronica put her leash on and held tight. You could never be too careful. She opened the door and almost fainted. Melody was breathtaking. She wore a long, many-layered white gown, a jeweled crown, and had silk flowers braided in her hair.

Fitzy chomped down on the hem of Melody's gown. No one noticed until the animal began swinging her head back and forth, violently, like she had a stuffed animal in her mouth she was trying to kill.

"Oh! Melody! Don't let her do that!" Mrs. Jenkins said.

"I'm not doing anything!" Melody cried.

Veronica was horrified. It was a matter of seconds before Melody's whole costume would be in tatters. She'd be naked.

"Fitzy! Drop it," Veronica commanded. She pulled Fitzy closer. Poor Fitzy. Her costume, which Veronica had worked so hard on, was awful compared to Melody's. "Your dress is so pretty, Melody," Veronica said, trying to reattach Fitzy's veil. "Are you a bride?"

"Sort of. I'm Adalgisa," Melody said, beaming. Veronica had never seen Melody so happy.

"I am sure she doesn't know who that is," Melody's mother said from the vestibule. She sounded embarrassed. Whether about the lavish costume her daughter was wearing or that Veronica had no idea who Adalgisa was, Veronica couldn't be sure.

"Adalgisa is the high priestess from Bellini's *Norma*," Melody explained.

"Oh," Veronica said.

Mrs. Jenkins, meanwhile, had backed away from the front door and was covering her mouth and nose with her scarf. "Melody," she said, her voice muffled, "your dad and I will pick you up downstairs at *nine p.m.* sharp. Okay?"

"Okay," Melody said.

Mrs. Morgan sauntered in from the living room. Why couldn't she just walk in and meet Veronica's friends like a normal person? That was obviously her own form of social anxiety. "Hello, I'm Marion Morgan. Come in! We've heard so much about Melody."

"I am extremely allergic to dogs," Mrs. Jenkins said.

"Oh no!" Mrs. Morgan said. "And we have two tonight!"

That information sent Melody's mother several feet farther away, and when the elevator doors opened she couldn't get inside fast enough. They waved goodbye and the elevator doors closed. That was the end of Mrs. Jenkins.

"This is very special for me. To be here. With you? I will shower for twenty minutes when I get home to remove the allergens from my body," Melody said.

"Oh my," Mrs. Morgan said. "Well, what a beautiful costume! Marvin, come look." Mr. Morgan appeared, making high-pitched sounds, which Veronica could only assume were meant to express delight.

"Oh! The opera friend! That is really a terrific costume! Just wonderful!" Marvin said. He encased Melody's fragile hands inside one of his enormous ones. "Pleasure to meet you, Melanie."

"Daddy, her name is Melody."

"That's what I said. Didn't I?"

"No, you said Melanie."

Mr. Morgan looked sheepishly at his wife for corroboration.

"You did. You called her Melanie," she said.

"My name is Melody," Melody said. "Melody Jenkins."

"Yes, dear, most of us know that," Mrs. Morgan said.

Minutes later Veronica opened the door for Sarah-Lisa and Athena. She was confused. They both seemed to be stuffed into a pair of khakis and a giant sweatshirt.

"We're *conjoined twins*," Sarah-Lisa said. "No one gets it, Athena. Why don't people understand us?"

Veronica looked more carefully. Athena and Sarah-Lisa were wearing one costume between them. One oversize hoodie and one three-legged pair of pants. They were still getting used to their new girth and struggled to fit through the door. They thought this was hilarious. When they finally pushed their way in, they knocked Veronica into the hall table. Everything on it fell to the floor: keys, mail, magazines, and dog leashes. Sarah-Lisa and Athena apologized, promising to pick everything up.

"Sarah-Lisa!" Athena cried. "You have to bend with me! One, two, three . . . bend," she said. But they were so giddy, all they could do was laugh.

Veronica had invited them, hoping this night would cement their friendship, but they showed up as *one person.* How much more left out could they make her feel?

"Athena, we are being so rude," Sarah-Lisa said. She flashed a perfect smile and shook Veronica's mother's hand. "I'm Sarah-Lisa Carver. Such a pleasure to be here."

"What a costume!" Mrs. Morgan said. "How did you do that? Do you mind if I stare?"

"No. That's the idea. We *want* to be stared at," Athena said.

Mrs. Morgan laughed and walked all the way around the two girls with her eyes and mouth wide.

Athena and Sarah-Lisa explained to Mrs. Morgan in too much detail how they had taken two large pairs of khakis and joined the two inside legs creating one three-legged pair. Veronica thought it was too perfect—a professional must have done it. She was fuming. Sarah-Lisa described the way they had put their inside arms around each other, while wrapping their torsos with a big Ace bandage until their upper bodies were united. Who cared! They went on to say how they put themselves inside the giant hooded sweatshirt and zipped it up the middle. As if that wasn't obvious.

The toilet in the powder room flushed and Marvin

Morgan appeared. Veronica thought she was going to break out in hives.

"Ah," he said, beaming, "you must be Athena-Lisa?"

"That is so clever!" Athena declared. "That should be our new name, since we're now officially one person. Let's be Athena-Lisa."

"Girls," Mrs. Morgan said, possibly sensing Veronica's distress, "come in the living room. We have one little thing we want to do before we let you out there to get candy."

Melody, meanwhile, had been left alone with the dogs in the living room and was nearly in tears. Cadbury sat patiently at her feet and Fitzy quietly chewed on the hem of her dress.

"Fitzy! Leave it!" Veronica said and picked her up. She felt so bad for Melody.

"Wow, Melody! What a getup! You look so pretty," Athena said.

"Where did you get that?" Sarah-Lisa asked.

"I borrowed it from the costume shop. It is from a production we did last year. I hope they won't be mad your dog ate some of it?" she added nervously. Was Melody serious? Of course they would be mad.

"Oh my gosh! Is that Cadbury?" Athena cried. She ran over, pulling Sarah-Lisa behind. They banged, rather hard, into the coffee table. It seemed they were never going to remember they were attached. They burst into hysterical laughter yet again.

"Sarah-Lisa," Athena said, "look at how cute the dogs are! Look at their charming costumes!"

Sarah-Lisa didn't share Athena's enthusiasm.

"Okay, gather round," Mr. Morgan said. "We have a little Morgan tradition. I want to get a picture of you in your costumes before you go on your merry way."

The instruction manual for this particular camera promised it was easy enough for a five-year-old to master, but the average five-year-old was a genius with technology compared to Mr. Morgan. The practice pictures he'd taken earlier of Cadbury had come out entirely black.

"When I was your age," he said, squinting into the camera, "we had to wait a week for the drugstore to get the film developed, and now there isn't even film. Okay, I have the lens thingy off. Let's try this."

Veronica found it incredible that her father had a job, considering he barely knew how to operate a camera, let alone a computer.

"Yep, I remember going to the drugstore and ripping open that envelope. I couldn't wait to see those pictures. Now you get impatient waiting a few seconds for the image to download on the whosie. Incredible. Everything is so different. Absolutely incredible. All you have to do now is push a button and the entire universe is available."

"It's a new world, Marvin, for the people who know which button to push," Veronica's mother said.

"*Daddy*, take the picture already." Veronica held the dogs tightly.

"One question before I shoot. You don't want to make it a Jewish wedding, Veronica? Your mother and I could go with you and carry a little chuppah, Cadbury could break a glass?" her father asked. "I just don't understand why the New Testament."

"Would it make you feel better if she was holding an Old Testament?" her mother said. Veronica cringed.

"Yes," her father said. "It would. I can't help it."

"You realize, Marvin, that for an atheist who hates religion, you make no sense," her mother said. Veronica caught Athena and Sarah-Lisa smirking.

"I am a very complex person, what can I say?"

"*Daddy*, take the picture, please!"

"Okay, ready? Here goes. Where's the whatsit?"

"Here, Marvin, push here," Marion Morgan said as his finger fumbled at the buttons.

Veronica held her breath and prayed he would take the shot so they could all get out of there.

Sometimes people gave out crummy stuff like pretzels or cheap lollipops that weren't even Tootsie Pops. But this year the candy was excellent and as apartment 12C's door closed, Veronica happily put three mini Snickers in her bag. They got into the elevator, en route to their final floor.

Athena made kissy noises at Fitzy. Since eating Melody's costume, Fitzy had been the picture of civility. She stood quietly next to Cadbury as if they were actually recently married.

"You know what? Those dogs are really cute," Sarah-Lisa said.

Just like that, every bad thought Veronica had ever had about Sarah-Lisa flew away. She stood next to Sarah-Lisa Carver, beaming.

"I want to take pictures," Sarah-Lisa said. "Veronica, you stand next to Fitzy? Melody, can you pick up Cadbury? Will someone take my picture with the dogs?" Veronica took the camera from Sarah-Lisa and snapped a few pictures. Sarah-Lisa let Cadbury lick her on the mouth. Athena egged her on and was in the picture too. This was as good as it could get. Veronica was thrilled.

"Are we moving?" Melody asked.

"Let me take some," Athena said. She took the camera. Sarah-Lisa put her arm around Veronica and they posed for a three-way selfie.

"You guys," Melody said, "I think the elevator is stuck."

Veronica listened for the whoosh that meant air was moving through the elevator shaft. But she couldn't hear anything over all the laughing from Sarah-Lisa and Athena.

"Shush, I'm trying to listen," she said. There hadn't been any jolt or bump or any noise to indicate there was a problem. But she'd been so lost in the picture taking and her new love for Sarah-Lisa she hadn't been paying attention.

Melody began hyperventilating. Veronica tried to calculate how long it had been since the doors closed on the twelfth floor, but she couldn't.

"Veronica, what kind of crazy elevator is this?" Sarah-Lisa said, frantically hitting buttons.

"Don't hit the buttons. That might make it worse," Veronica said. She had no idea if it would or not. But if she was an elevator, and she was stuck, she would not appreciate being hit and banged upon.

"I knew something exciting would happen on the bad-luck floor. We're stuck on thirteen. It's so romantic," Athena said.

"What is romantic about dying on Halloween, Athena?" Sarah-Lisa said. "Melody, are you going to faint? Eat this piece of chocolate. Seriously, you look like you are going to pass out. It's going to be okay. Right, Veronica?"

Veronica had no idea if everything was going to be okay and if Sarah-Lisa hadn't just made her responsible for making everything okay, she probably would have been hysterical. But now that she was responsible she had to stay calm.

She picked up the red EMERGENCY telephone. It was Charlie. She was so happy to hear his voice. "I think the elevator is stuck," Veronica said.

"Copy," Charlie said. "All right. I see you on the control board, you're on fourteen. I'm going to have to reboot the system. Do you see the button on the lower left panel? It looks like a hammer?"

"Yes," Veronica said.

She looked at her friends, whose lives she was suddenly responsible for. She hoped she was up to the job. Mary always said something about faking it till you make it. She tried to exude a sense of authority, like she rebooted elevators all the time.

"Keep watching and tell me when it turns green." Veronica's pulse beat along with the flashing hammer. "Is it green?" Charlie asked. The button went dark like it had died. Veronica checked to see if she had died too. She was still breathing, but barely. Melody was white as a sheet.

"This is so fun!" Athena said. "Maybe we'll have to sleep in here. Maybe we'll have to miss school. Maybe they'll call in a news crew."

Veronica stared hard at the button. It was still unlit. She was afraid to blink in case she missed something. A symbol she hadn't seen before appeared. "Charlie, it just changed. It's green."

"Wonderful. Hold it down at the same time as the reset button on the left. Use two hands if you can't reach. Keep them down together and don't let up until I tell you. I will tell you when to let go."

"Okay," Veronica said. She stretched her fingers so she could put her left thumb on the reset button and her index finger on the green button. She had small hands, but she did it.

"You scared?" Charlie asked.

"No," Veronica lied.

"You're doing great. Tell me when you feel motion."

They waited for a jolt, for something that would indicate they weren't stuck anymore. But they didn't feel anything. "Nothing is happening, Charlie," Veronica said, trying to hide her panic.

"Hang on," Charlie said.

They were hanging on. But they didn't have any water. And only so much oxygen. How long before they breathed up all the air in there? There were four of them, after all, plus dogs.

There was a rattle and a clank and a whoosh. The doors opened and they were on the twelfth floor.

"Yay! We are back on the twelfth floor, Charlie!" Veronica said. She couldn't believe it, but it was true.

"Good girl, all should be fine now. Bring candy. Over."

Veronica and Melody burst into the lobby raining candy on Charlie like confetti. Veronica made him take her one full-size Snickers and Melody tried to give him her whole bag.

"Help!" Athena screamed. Not only were she and

Sarah-Lisa one person, they had to be one person who couldn't function without making everyone look at them. "Does anyone have scissors? A nail file? I can't stand it anymore! I have to get out of this costume," she said.

Nothing would have made Veronica happier than producing a pair of scissors!

Athena and Sarah-Lisa attacked their costume like animals, using their nails and teeth until the zipper gave, exposing the bandage that held them together. They burst out of the elevator free and laughing hysterically.

The night was over and Cadbury was snoring quietly next to Veronica, but she couldn't fall asleep. She should have been happy. She hadn't died in the elevator. She'd gotten everyone out safely and hadn't disappointed any of the people who had wanted to trick-or-treat with her.

But even though Sarah-Lisa and Athena's twin costume had ripped at the seams, their friendship never would. She was destined to be the outsider. They made it look like there was room for other people, but Veronica knew she would never get inside.

End of Days

Thanksgiving was so delicious Veronica wished they could eat turkey basted with maple syrup and ancho pepper every day. She loved pouring her mother's gravy over everything. Mary's stuffing with apples and sausages was the best thing in the world. And why was pumpkin pie something people only had at Thanksgiving? The whole family and a few close friends feasted till their stomachs burst.

The following Saturday Veronica and her mother left early. They went to their favorite café on Lexington, had hot chocolate and croissants, window-shopped along Madison, and walked to Second Avenue to choose their Christmas tree from the same man who drove in from Vermont every year. This was their tradition.

A particularly scrawny tree called to them. It was a tree that was the underdog, a tree no one else would want. Taking turns, they dragged it home. By the time they reached Fifth Avenue, their hands were raw and covered in sticky sap. It was a perfect day except for the weather. Buying a Christmas tree in unseasonably warm sixty-seven-degree weather was not right. It should have been cold with at least a threat of snow.

"I can't believe we had hot chocolate this morning!" Mrs. Morgan said. "I'm ready for iced tea now."

"Or ice cream," Veronica said, wiping sweat from her face.

"Ice cream! Maybe we'll make egg creams when we get home. Hey, do you remember where I put the decorations last year?" her mother asked.

"The front closet?" Veronica guessed.

"Gosh, I hope not." No one liked to go in the front closet, lest something fall on them. "I think maybe they're in the back of the linen closet. Mary took out the stand yesterday, bless her."

Charlie saw them coming down the block and ran to their aid. He picked up the tree and swung it over his shoulder.

"This is some tree," he said, smiling. "Where is the rest of it?"

"You'll see," Mrs. Morgan said. "With a little attention, this tree will look wonderful."

She brought the stand out to the living room and she and Veronica were busy struggling with the screws when Mr. Morgan walked in.

"What in the name of, Marion! Why? Why?"

"Marvin, please don't start," his wife said.

"What the hell is a nice Jewish family doing with a bloody Christmas tree? *I don't understand!*"

"Because it smells good," Mrs. Morgan replied. "And it's pretty. Okay, Veronica, tighten your screw."

Veronica did, and each turn filled the living room with more scent from their aromatic pine tree. When the trunk was secured they filled the bottom of the stand with water and stood back to admire their sweet, pathetic tree.

Cadbury approved by curling up underneath it.

"Daddy," Veronica said. "What's wrong with celebrating what makes you happy, regardless of what religion you are? Isn't it like eating Sephardic charosis at Passover? We aren't Sephardic, right? Plus, didn't you tell the Lubavitchers on the street yesterday you weren't Jewish? Because if you're not Jewish, then who cares if we have a tree? And even if we are, who cares?"

Mrs. Morgan laughed. "You realize, Marvin, that you make absolutely no sense whatsoever."

"Well, neither do you. With the shivas and the Christmas trees and the challah and the Christmas cookies."

"I make sense to myself," Mrs. Morgan said.

Logically Veronica understood what her father was saying. But her mother was the one who made sense.

* * *

The December wind whipped through the trees so fiercely that Veronica wondered if there would be any leaves left on the branches by the time she and Cadbury got back from their afternoon walk. Although *walk* was a stretch. Lately Cadbury refused to move after his leash was on and Veronica had to carry him in and out of the elevator.

"He's on strike, huh?" Charlie said. He had on his winter uniform, which included gold shoulder tassels. Veronica wondered if he liked it. It sure was fancy. She offered Cadbury a slow-baked sweet potato chip, hoping to lure him out of the elevator. Mary had invented that particular treat on one of the many days she'd forgotten she didn't like dogs.

"Where is his other half?" Charlie said.

"Florida until April, remember? Fitzy always goes right before the holidays," Veronica said.

"Right you are. Right you are. Maybe you need to get your fellow on the first flight. Looks like he misses his lady. Let me get the door for you, my dear," Charlie said.

A burst of cool air rushed at her and Veronica wondered what it was like being Charlie. Having a job that made you stay in your coat all day long, inside. Veronica imagined she would be uncomfortable, but it never seemed to bother him.

Poor Cadbury shivered. She was a negligent owner. Fitzy had a coat, a sweater, and sometimes Mrs. Ferguson even put Fitzy in little shoes. Fitzy probably had a new coat just for Miami. A monogrammed windbreaker.

"I am ordering you a coat, Cadbury. Something very fashionable. Maybe with toggles." The thought of him in a toggle coat made her happy. "Fitzy will be jealous when she comes back."

The wind went right through her open hoodie, so she pulled both sides together in an attempt to keep it closed. Cadbury had chewed out the zipper. She should have worn a real coat, but the cold weather had come out of nowhere and she refused to dress for it.

The leaves blew high and in flurries and she felt like she was in a snow globe. Soon the air would smell like fireplaces and pine needles and toasted marshmallows, like real winter. Veronica didn't mind winter. The only thing she couldn't manage was how early it got dark. Night at four o'clock in the afternoon always felt like the beginning of the end.

"Why are you being so poky?" Veronica asked her dog. Cadbury replied by sighing loudly.

"Are you crabby about daylight saving time too? I don't blame you but the slower you walk, the longer it will take us to get to the park and the less daylight we'll have."

Her argument did not convince Cadbury. He was practically nailed to the sidewalk.

Veronica reminded herself of what Mrs. Harrison said

yesterday, that moods are formed in the mind. If that was true, she'd better form a new mood before she got mad at Cadbury. They weren't really in a hurry. She'd already finished her homework. The leaves crunched under Veronica's feet.

She thought of the chestnut poem from the first week at Randolf. Where did things begin and end? Leaves fell and became part of the ground they landed on. The ground nourished another tree, which produced nuts, which were then eaten by a bird or a squirrel who would poop and fertilize another tree and so on and so forth.

Nature, Veronica concluded for about the hundredth time since getting Cadbury, was helpful to all living things. *Maybe that's why I used to rub my fingers up and down my green carpet so much. I just needed a little patch of Central Park.* She wrapped the soft lining of her sweatshirt gently around her finger as if she could protect it from all the years of rug burn.

"Look!" Veronica said. She picked up what was obviously the world's best stick. But when she threw it, Cadbury lay down.

"Did you forget how it's done? Here, let me show you. Watch."

Cadbury tried to get comfortable in the leaves as Veronica fetched the stick herself. She returned with it, but Cadbury just looked at her.

“You’re not going to play with me?” she asked.

When it was clear that he wasn’t, Veronica played fetch by herself. She ran back and forth until she collapsed next to Cadbury.

For years Mary had told Veronica she would make another friend besides Cricket Cohen and Veronica hadn’t believed her. But that was because the friend Veronica had tried to imagine was human, not canine. She gently covered her new friend Cadbury with a blanket of leaves. She lay next to him, staring up at the sky with its last little bit of daylight.

Doctor-in-Training Esme Weiner

Ten minutes later, Veronica pushed through the front door of Paws and Claws carrying Cadbury, who was wrapped in her sweatshirt.

"Ohhhh, Cadbury! Come to Esme. I missed you," Esme said, rushing out from behind the counter. She nearly mowed them down in her excitement. "Oh. You are so sweet. You are so sweet. You are so sweet." She tickled Cadbury under his chin and massaged his glorious ears. Cadbury licked Esme all over.

"Hey, Veronica," Ray muttered.

"Hi," Veronica answered. It still surprised her that she and Ray were now on speaking terms. Being a verified dog owner gave her credibility. She was no longer just a desperate child begging her parents for permission to own a pet. She owned a pet so she had every right to be there. Even Simon couldn't make her feel bad.

As usual, Ray wasn't even pretending to work. His head rested on a giant bag of kibble. He stared dreamily into space while the radio played a song about booties and girls and good times. Veronica felt sorry for Ray. He must miss Esme now that she interned so much at the vet's office. But he would never admit it.

"He's all winded. And he's shivering," Esme said, her face burrowed in Cadbury's fur. "Listen."

"Uh-oh," Ray said, "doctor-in-training Esme Weiner with another doggie diagnostic prediction of doom." Ray lifted his head from the kibble. "Veronica, you are probably not feeding him some important organical plant supplement or exercising him enough or whatever. Whatever you're doing, the doctor here has a better idea."

"Ray, shut up."

"You shut up."

"Veronica, for real," Esme said, ignoring Ray, "come here and listen."

Veronica put her ear against Cadbury's chest. She heard a kind of rattling.

"He shouldn't be doing that," Esme said. "His breathing seems weird. If you don't mind, I want to call Dr. Harskirey and make an appointment."

Ray got up off his kibble and put his arm around Veronica. "Leave the kid alone," he said. "You're gonna scare her and you're not even a doctor, or a vet, or whatever."

It was nice to have Ray looking out for her. But she let Esme call Dr. Harskirey because even though she wanted Esme to be wrong, she was afraid she was right.

Symmetry and Percentages

"Even his bones are beautiful," Veronica said.

She stood beside her mother, gazing at Cadbury's X-rays. His guitar-shaped rib cage was lit from behind. Veronica herself had only been subjected to X-rays at the dentist's office. It was hard to believe that a little dog could have had more medical procedures than its owner. Cadbury had undergone an alarming number of tests in the last twenty-four hours.

Dr. Harskirey walked in and snapped on the overhead lights. She was taller than Veronica's mother, with wild gray hair that seemed to be fighting a losing battle for control of the ponytail it was half contained by. She was direct, abrupt, and nervous making. Veronica didn't like her.

"May I speak in front of the child?" Dr. Harskirey said. Veronica didn't understand how Esme could admire her so much. She seemed so unpleasant.

"Her name is Veronica, Dr. Harskirey," Mrs. Morgan said. "I believe I introduced you yesterday. And today, actually."

"I'm sorry," Dr. Harskirey said. She turned toward Veronica and extended her enormous hand. It was strong and the veins on top were ropy and prominent. She wasn't smiling. "Veronica," she said, "I'm going to be straight with you. The news is not good, and I need to know if you would be more comfortable having your mom explain Cadbury's diagnosis at home later, or would you like to listen to me run through a long list of doctor talk?"

Veronica looked at her mother for guidance.

"Would you give us a moment?" Veronica's mother said.

"Certainly," Dr. Harskirey said.

"I'm sorry. I meant alone. Would you please give us a moment alone." Mrs. Morgan stroked her daughter's cheek.

Dr. Harskirey looked at her watch. "I have other patients. If I walk out there I can pretty much promise I won't be back in anytime soon."

Veronica sensed her mother losing her temper. Her own pulse was racing and she hoped her mother's neck wasn't going to explode from tension.

"I certainly don't want to make trouble, Dr. Harskirey," Mrs. Morgan said, "but I have to tell you that your bedside manner . . . well, it stinks!" Mrs. Morgan wiped a tear from her eye. "Could you try to put yourself in our shoes, in Veronica's shoes, for a minute? I would be so grateful."

Veronica loved her mother for defending her and Dr. Harskirey actually apologized. Mrs. Morgan pulled Veronica close, wrapping her arms around her the way she did if it was cold and they were outside for too long. "What would you rather, honey? Hear Dr. Harskirey explain the situation or have me do it at home?"

Her voice was respectful, the way Veronica preferred being spoken to ordinarily. But today she wanted a mother who knew more than she did. A mother who would take care of everything and make it better.

"Lovey, what do you think?"

Veronica stared at her mother like a mute.

Dr. Harskirey shifted her weight and looked at her watch.

"Honey? She has other patients. Let's let her explain."

Veronica nodded and leaned into her mother. She smelled so good.

"Okay. Here we go," Dr. Harskirey said. She put more X-rays up on the board. "Cadbury's tests confirm what I was worried about yesterday. His heart is enlarged. It's putting pressure on the lungs. The entire cardiopulmonary system is backing up with fluid . . ."

Dr. Harskirey seemed to lose track of what she was saying. "I . . . I want to draw your attention to the large mass in the center." She pointed her finger at a gray blotch surrounded by small white bones. "That is Cadbury's heart. Do you see how big it is?"

Yesterday when Dr. Harskirey said she suspected that

Cadbury's heart was enlarged, Veronica took it as a compliment. The larger the heart, she reasoned, the kinder the creature. The size of a heart must be proportionate to how lovable the being containing that heart was. Obviously Cadbury had the biggest heart in the world. Veronica didn't need years of medical training and a set of X-rays to know that.

"Cadbury, as I suspected, has an abnormally large heart," Dr. Harskirey continued. Veronica picked Cadbury up off the floor. His breath was hot against her cheek.

"According to his echocardiogram and the X-rays—I don't have a nice way to say this, I wish I did. And I don't have a script that is more appropriate for certain age groups." Dr. Harskirey took Cadbury from Veronica and put him on the aluminum table. His nails made an upsetting sound as they skittered across it. It seemed wrong for this rude woman to be touching Cadbury. But she was surprisingly gentle with him. He licked Dr. Harskirey's nose. She smiled and scratched behind his ears. "Basically, his heart is too large to do the job it is supposed to do."

"How can a heart be too big?" Veronica asked.

"That is the problem," Dr. Harskirey said. "It can't. His body is designed to contain a much smaller heart. And his heart is designed to be much smaller. It's working too hard to pump all the blood his body needs. That's why he is having trouble breathing. That's why he coughs. That's why he is so tired. You've probably noticed he's not playful." Cadbury's heart glowed on the light box behind Dr. Harskirey. "Eventually all his organs will suffer. I wish there was a nicer way. I really do," Dr. Harskirey said, stroking Cadbury's chin.

Cadbury didn't seem to mind Dr. Harskirey or what she was saying. Veronica wished she felt the same way.

"Some dogs are diagnosed early and some dogs, like Cadbury, show no signs until their hearts have built up so much fluid the damage is irreversible. You didn't do anything wrong. It is a hereditary condition most of the time."

"Veronica," her mother said quietly, "do you understand?"

"Yes," Veronica answered. "Cadbury's heart is too big and it makes him tired."

Veronica had a math test first thing in the morning. She should be at home studying. It was about symmetry, which was easy, but there was a section on percentages, which was hard.

"What is the treatment?" her mother said.

"In Cadbury's case all we can do is keep him comfortable."

"That's it?" Veronica felt her mother's arms tighten around her. She thought she might choke.

"I'm afraid so," Dr. Harskirey said. "He is quite far gone, and it is just going to get worse."

"What do you mean?" Veronica asked. "He is just going to get more tired?"

"Yes. And then his heart will give out. Or if you feel he is too uncomfortable you may decide to euthanize him."

"Honey, look at me," Mrs. Morgan said, turning Veronica to face her. "Do you understand what the doctor is saying?"

"Yes," Veronica said. She was annoyed. "Yes, I do. Cadbury's heart is too big and he will be tired and not as playful for the rest of his life."

Cadbury was always going to die. She was going to die. Her mother and father were going to die. It was all part of the cycle of life, the seasons of the year like they talked about at Randolf. The leaves fall off the trees, the ground freezes, the earth hibernates waiting to be reborn in spring and it all culminates in the bounty of summer. Blah blah blah.

Mrs. Morgan was crying. Her poor mother always overreacted. All those years spent forcing herself to be sympathetic, even when nothing was going on. If only she made a big deal out of stuff that actually mattered. Like getting school uniforms tailored properly and cooking for her family.

"You should get a second opinion," Dr. Harskirey said.

"We will. Thank you. But from what I see on the X-rays and what I remember from medical school, I can't imagine it will be much different. How much time do you think he has, Dr. Harskirey?"

"It's hard to say. I will prescribe some medications to reduce the inflammation and relax the heart muscle, but frankly I'm surprised he's made it this long. Right now it is all about keeping him comfortable."

A burst of cold air slapped Veronica in the face as they stepped outside the vet's office.

"Honey, pull your hat down. I don't want you to catch a cold," Mrs. Morgan said. She fiddled with Veronica's hat and hailed a taxi. "Where are your gloves? Please say you didn't lose them."

"Can we not talk about my stupid gloves!" Veronica snapped.

"Don't yell at me, Veronica. I feel as bad as you do," her mother said.

No, you don't, Veronica thought, *nobody feels as bad as I do.* But she didn't say anything. She just held on to Cadbury as tightly as possible.

Colors

"It's hard to imagine how radical these paintings were when they first appeared," Ms. Padgett said the following day in main lesson. They were doing a unit about the Impressionists. "Painting motion and life and nuance instead of stationary objects in the act of being perfectly still was really bold! The Impressionists took the rules of composition and form and *ignored* them. They dedicated themselves to perceiving more elusive subjects like light."

A week earlier Ms. Padgett had showed the class a slide of Monet's *Women in the Garden*. It was a beautiful scene. A woman ran around a tree, another woman smelled flowers, and another sat on the grass.

"It's important to remember that, although now the Impressionists are household names, at the time, they were the oddballs. Many critics mocked their work because they dared to see the world in an unconventional, newly observed way."

The lights in the classroom were off and the shades were drawn and Veronica was miles away. Ms. Padgett must have noticed because she addressed Veronica directly when she said, "Girls, it is almost always the oddballs of the world who make a difference. The people who fit in, the people who are like everyone else, may be popular, but they are not the ones who rewrite history."

The only history Veronica wanted to rewrite was Cadbury's. It was hard to imagine thinking about anything beyond her own circumstances. If Veronica could change Cadbury's fate, that would be plenty. She didn't need to change the world.

At the end of class, Ms. Padgett assigned projects. "You are all deep thinkers and I want you to explore how these paintings work emotionally and respond with your own piece of art." Veronica had probably failed her symmetry test that morning, so she was grateful to have another chance.

"Go to the museum and look at Monet's gardens, the haystacks, the water lilies, whatever moves you. You have two weeks to create an original work of art. A piece of music, an essay, a painting of your own—the medium is less important than the expression of an idea. I'm pairing you. You can work as a team or just use each other to bounce ideas off of."

Veronica and Melody were paired. Melody beamed.

And as soon as class was over she cornered her. "I'm so excited. My parents are so strict about playdates, but we won't be playing. It will be academic. Let's work every day, okay? Can you come over this afternoon?"

Veronica hated to burst her bubble. "I can't, Melody. My dog is sick. I have to go home."

The project sounded fun in theory, but trips to the museum or to Melody's house would be impossible. Cadbury needed her every afternoon, every night. The assignment was going to be a disaster.

Scrabble

Mary drank a cup of tea and put down a plate of Oreos. Veronica relaxed for the first time all day. Cadbury was resting his head on her lap, and life was livable. "Scrabble?" Mary suggested. Veronica was thrilled to oblige. She covered Cadbury with a quilt and gently twirled his ears while Mary unfolded the board and threw down the letters.

"Mary, tell me about your family," Veronica said. Mary's family had lived through World War II. There weren't many of them left and the subject was usually off-limits. But under the circumstances, Veronica hoped Mary would bend. She felt like traveling somewhere that wasn't here or now.

"Oh, my baby. That was a long time ago. And very far away. You know I don't like to talk about it. It lives in me. That is enough." Mary looked up and smiled a sad smile. "I made him some livers today. Just like my mother used to make. Good for his heart. He is eating, that is a good sign."

Unlike her parents, Mary didn't make Veronica talk about anything. Veronica fiddled with her Scrabble letters and arranged the word *r-a-d-i-u-s* on the board. Thirty-one points. It was a decent word, not a fancy word, but it utilized the triple word score. Mary, for all her infinite wisdom and kindness, had never mastered triple and double word scores. Veronica nearly always won.

"You know what I do, my baby, when I am worried?"

"What?" Veronica asked. She tried to relax her face so she didn't look worried.

"I remind myself that I am loved. Don't make a face and tell me it is cornmeal."

"Corny."

"Nothing is all the way bad when there is that. It is a shelf. To catch you from falling all the way down. I love you. Your parents love you very much. Cadbury loves you. Look how he loves you. And he is right there, still breathing, very much alive, on your lap. It is too soon to worry, my baby."

Mary spelled *t-o-y* and got six points. "It is your turn, my baby," Mary said.

Veronica carefully removed her hand, which had been resting under Cadbury's barrel chest and had fallen asleep. She shook it, and the dog gave a sigh. Mary was right. It was too soon to worry. She looked back at her letters. She had a *J*. The word *j-o-y* came to mind. But there was no place to make that word with the letters on the board arranged the way they were. And even if there was, *j-o-y* was hardly worth the measly thirteen points.

"Do you have homework, my baby?" Mary asked.

"No," Veronica lied. She couldn't very well work on her Monet project if she wasn't at the museum. Tomorrow she would go to the museum. Tomorrow she would deal with Melody because tomorrow Cadbury would be better. Tomorrow he would need her less.

Noodle Art

It had been five days since Dr. Harskirey's diagnosis and four days since the Impressionist project had been assigned. Veronica was so focused on Cadbury she hadn't met with Melody once. Cadbury was taking three medications now. One had to be administered on an empty stomach and two had to be taken with food. Veronica made a schedule and a calendar and took it upon herself to mark off each dose. His medication was supposed to make him more comfortable, but it seemed to make him exhausted. He slept practically all the time.

"I hate that vet," Mrs. Morgan said at dinner. "She's like a surgeon: all skill and no heart. Oh, I don't know what we are going to do."

"Veronica, do you agree with your mother? What do you think of Dr. Harskirwhoosie?" Mr. Morgan passed his wife the lamb.

"I don't know," Veronica said. She was absently twirling

lo mein on her fork and then turning her fork in the opposite direction so the noodles all fell off.

"How are you, honey?" her mother asked. "When I'm sad I overeat. Aren't you hungry?"

"Not really."

"Well, you're lucky. I will probably blow up like a balloon on top of everything. This has been an awful week." Mrs. Morgan blew her nose into her napkin and started to cry.

"A terrible time," her father echoed.

It was a terrible time but, truth be told, her mother's feelings were taking up all the room. Veronica figured she would wait until her mother calmed down. Maybe then her own feelings could come to the surface. For now she put her bare feet on top of Cadbury, who was half-asleep under her chair.

"It's a lot to process." Her mother wiped her nose. "Do you have any questions, honey? Anything you'd like to talk about? Talking really helps."

"It is really a big blow. There is so much to talk about. Marion, pass that wonderful green dish, will you?"

"What can we do? We want to help you," her mother said. Mr. Morgan got up from his chair and put his arms around his wife, who was crying uncontrollably.

"Oh, I'm a mess!" Mrs. Morgan said, honking her nose like an old goose. "I wish I had your composure, lovey." She blew her nose into a wad of Kleenex.

Veronica didn't know what to say. She was with her parents, surrounded by familiar white cardboard takeout containers, doing what they did best—eating Chinese food—but she felt alone and frightened. If only she hadn't taken Cadbury to see Esme in the first place. She wedged one of her feet under Cadbury. His body kept her feet warm, even though he couldn't seem to keep himself warm. No matter where he was in the house, in front of a radiator, on his fleecy dog bed, or wrapped in a blanket, he shivered.

"Veronica, are you sure you wouldn't like to talk about anything?" Mr. Morgan asked.

"No, I don't want to talk about anything," Veronica said. "May I be excused?" She couldn't sit there with them for another second. Not that she had anywhere better to go.

She lifted Cadbury into bed. She followed the outline of his spots, tracing them with her finger. There were five of them. Five distinct caramel islands in a sea of white. She made a little boat with her finger and took a trip in the ocean of his white fur.

"Where shall we travel, Cadbury? Where will we be happy?" Cadbury looked into Veronica's eyes and she looked back into his.

Poor Melody

Melody cared so much about grades and Veronica was sick with guilt for letting her down about the project. She hadn't met with her once, which was pretty much the worst thing you could do to Melody, other than criticize her singing voice or opera in general. Veronica knew she needed to apologize. She waited all morning until Melody was alone by her locker.

"Hi, Melody," Veronica said.

"Are you mad at me?" Melody asked.

"Melody, no. I'm not mad at you," Veronica said.

"My mother doesn't think you're a good friend," Melody said. "She thinks you're letting me do all the work."

"I am. I'm sorry," was all Veronica could muster. This conversation wasn't relieving her of guilt. If anything, it was making it worse. And poor Melody had it all wrong. Veronica wasn't the one who was mad. Melody was the one who should be mad but she was so nice, she blamed herself. Veronica had become the Cricket Cohen to Melody Jenkins's Veronica. It was horrible.

"What gives, you guys?" Sarah-Lisa said. "Veronica, you have been, like, totally antisocial. Right, Athena?"

"What have you been doing, Veronica? Do you have a secret life?" Athena asked. There was an awkward silence.

"Um," Melody said uncertainly, "that's what we were just talking about."

"Yeah," Veronica said.

"Well, what's with you?" Sarah-Lisa asked.

"Cadbury might be sick."

"Oh no," Athena said. "My mom was really sick last week."

Athena and Sarah-Lisa went into Mr. Bower's room for science. Nothing was going the way she wanted it to go. "Melody," Veronica finally said, "you shouldn't count on me. You should turn the project in as your own. I can't do it with you."

She thought clarifying that would make things better, but Melody looked like she'd been punched in the stomach.

Signs

In Veronica's mind, if Dr. Harskirey's diagnosis was true, she and her mother would have left the office that afternoon and the world outside would have been altered. Radically. News that big had to change things. But the doormen still dotted Fifth Avenue in their colorful regalia just like always. The homeless man was still asleep on his regular bench on 103rd Street. Everything continued the next day and every day after as though nothing had happened. The food cart on Ninety-Sixth Street served the same stumbling early-morning crowd. Men and women clutched butter-stained bagel bags and cardboard cups of steaming coffee. Athena and Sarah-Lisa still wore matching cardigan sets, Melody was still in the children's chorus trying her hand at popularity, and Sylvie was still pulling spines out of fish carcasses. The sky hadn't split open hurling black snow to the ground, there were no flying elephants, there were no frogs leaping from faucets, no tigers stalking Central Park, not a single symbol to corroborate the horrible event Dr. Harskirey said was coming.

Veronica looked everywhere. She didn't find it, so she concluded that Dr. Harskirey was wrong and that her parents were wrong to believe her. She chose to believe that Cadbury, like everything everywhere else in the world, was the same as before.

All she had to do was believe that everything would be okay and it would be okay. It wasn't easy, but it's what Morning Meeting had prepared her for: replace a negative with a positive. She had never been more determined to look at the bright side.

More Opinions

Mrs. Morgan didn't believe everything was fine and that nothing had changed. She took Cadbury for second and third opinions with veterinarian heart specialists named Dr. Humphreys and Dr. Adelman. Over moo shu chicken and orange beef Mr. Morgan inquired, "Do Humphreys and Adelman agree with Harskirey?"

"Yes."

"Shipt."

"It is awful," Mrs. Morgan said. "Please pass the dumplings and the Kleenex and don't curse at the dinner table." She blew her nose loudly and wiped more tears from her face.

"I didn't curse. I almost did. But I didn't."

"Oh, Marvin, it really seems to be just a matter of time."

"Your mother is quite a woman, you know that?" Mr. Morgan said, taking a dumpling before passing them on.

"Juggling her patients, a dying dog, and managing to get second and third opinions."

"Stop it!" Veronica said. The aggression in her voice surprised everyone. Including herself. But how dare they. All she had done for the last two weeks was try to protect Cadbury by thinking positive thoughts and here, in front of him, her parents were blatantly undermining her efforts.

"You're upset, honey. And you should be. This is so upsetting. It is so upsetting," her mother said. She got up from the table and came around to Veronica's chair.

"It really is so upsetting," her father said, and it wasn't clear if he was speaking to himself or to Veronica.

They didn't get it. She was Cadbury's antenna. She was responsible for bringing him home. He was tuned in to one station only and that station played the show called *Everything Is Fine and Nothing Has Changed.* Her parents were messing up the signal.

The next day, Melody handed in the Monet project and barely looked at Veronica. She was proud of Melody for that. Melody had written an essay and Veronica bet it would be very good. So now the job of exposing Veronica for the negligent student and bad school partner she was belonged to Ms. Padgett. Veronica watched the clock, waiting for the other shoe to drop. She wanted someone to get mad at her. When would Ms. Padgett announce she was a bad girl? There would be a heavy price to pay for her behavior.

It would hurt. She was ready.

But class was dismissed.

Devotion

Veronica quickly adjusted her expectations. She would get in trouble when the projects were handed back on Monday. It made perfect sense. Monday morning, she would go down like the *Titanic* while Melody was held up as an example of everything good. Veronica understood that getting kicked out of Randolf was a very real possibility. She should be kicked out. She had behaved like a scoundrel.

That weekend, Mr. and Mrs. Morgan had an out-of-town wedding so Mary stayed over. Veronica taught Mary how to bathe Cadbury. They cleared out the tub, removing the razors and combs and shampoo and conditioner so Cadbury could take a bath. Just as Esme would, Veronica adjusted and readjusted the temperature many times until it was perfect. She and Mary lifted him into the water and Veronica rubbed his body with rosemary oil to stimulate his circulation. She rinsed him carefully and rubbed him gently with lavender oil to soothe him. She dried him with her own towel.

"Here, my baby," Mary said, and handed Veronica a cup of hot chocolate. "You are taking such good care of your friend."

"Are you crying, Mary?"

"No. My baby, I am not crying," Mary said, wiping her face. "Something is in my eye. Should I be crying?"

"No. Because everything's going to be all right," Veronica said.

"That is right. Everything will be how it is meant to be," Mary said. She kissed Veronica before going back to the kitchen. But she only kissed her one time.

When Ms. Padgett handed back the projects a few days later, Veronica was in a panic.

"I had such a good time this week with your projects! Great work. And such a diverse display. I read poems and looked at pictures and I even heard a song," Ms. Padgett said. Auden Georges was on the edge of her chair. She'd made a watercolor and was really pleased with herself. "You should all be very proud," Ms. Padgett said as she glided around the room handing back the projects.

Veronica's finger itched like crazy. She rubbed it against her uniform. She had nothing to be proud of. Becky Shickler got her paper back and hugged Darcy. Ms. Padgett came to Veronica's table. Sylvie had written what looked like a dissertation. It was long and Ms. Padgett said, "Sylvie, this was so thought provoking. I loved how you wrote about

Monet painting his wife as she was dying." She put Sylvie's pages on the table. "Athena, wonderful work. You too, Sarah-Lisa." Ms. Padgett handed back their work. "Veronica," Ms. Padgett said and Veronica swallowed hard. "You and Melody worked so well together. Lovely." She placed a paper in front of Veronica with the names Melody Jenkins and Veronica Morgan printed across the top and a big red *A* in Ms. Padgett's loopy handwriting.

"You look surprised," Ms. Padgett said. "You shouldn't be. Hard work is rewarded in my class."

Veronica smiled weakly. Why had Melody let her get away with this? To torture her? Then it occurred to her. It was a sign. Instead of being punished for being mean to Melody, she was being rewarded for her devotion to Cadbury. Cadbury was the prize.

Closed Windows

When Veronica got home from school she was surprised to discover her parents.

"Why aren't you at work?"

"Your father and I have something difficult to discuss with you," Mrs. Morgan said. Cadbury lay limp at her feet.

"But what about your patients? Shouldn't you go back?"

"Veronica," her father said, "Mary told us Cadbury hasn't eaten for days."

"He isn't hungry. He is resting."

Mr. and Mrs. Morgan looked at each other as though they had this all planned out.

"Honey, I know it's hard. But it is time to start making arrangements," her mother said.

For three weeks Veronica had worked day and night maintaining a positive attitude. She always gave him his medicine at the right time. She fed him with a spoon when he was having trouble eating. She cleaned out his water bowl two or three times a day. She researched about rosemary and lavender oils. She bathed him so carefully. She had tried as hard as a person could try to protect him. But she had obviously failed. And now her parents were asking her to abandon hope. She looked into Cadbury's eyes but he didn't see her.

Darkness

The next day Veronica couldn't bear the idea of going to school. She stayed in bed with Cadbury until it was time to go to Dr. Harskirey's. At three thirty the sky was pitch-black as if all the daylight had been stolen from the heavens. It was the sign Veronica had been waiting for. Everything was not fine even though she had stayed the course, even though she had done her part, even though she had been good.

"Honey, he's too heavy. Let me carry him for you," her mother said when they got out of the taxi.

Not eating had made Cadbury both lighter and heavier than Veronica expected.

"Please, honey," her mother begged, "let me help you."

"No," Veronica said.

Cadbury sat on Veronica's lap while Esme helped her mother with the paperwork. Veronica wouldn't let herself cry because more than anything, she didn't want Cadbury to be afraid. This was the last thing she could give him. She would not let him die in fear and without honor. She kissed him gently everywhere on his body.

"I love you. I love you. I love you. You are the best dog in the world," Veronica told him over and over.

"Check cremation," Esme told Mrs. Morgan. "It is very important that Veronica keeps the ashes."

Veronica's mother did as instructed and brought Veronica a catalog of urns to look at. She stroked her daughter's hair much the way Veronica was stroking Cadbury.

"Honey, will you pick something for Cadbury?" she said softly.

Veronica was queasy like her first day of pre-K when she didn't understand how to do anything, even where to put her coat, until the teacher told her. She followed her mother's instructions now as she had followed the teacher's then. She chose a wooden box.

When the forms were finished, Esme led them to a special procedural room in the basement. It was a much warmer room than where Cadbury had been examined and there were three thick blankets draping the metal table. Veronica placed Cadbury gently in the middle of them. She lifted his ear and told him how much she loved him. She repeated it over and over while Esme held him and Dr. Harskirey shaved a little patch of fur on his leg. Veronica's mother held her daughter while Dr. Harskirey administered the injection. It took seven minutes.

They went to the vet with Cadbury and they left the vet without Cadbury. There was nothing to say. Veronica held on to her mother as though she were blind.

"I've got you," her mother said. She steered her daughter through the early evening streets. Veronica couldn't see beyond the giant drops of rain that were suddenly falling everywhere. She leaned into her mother and closed her eyes. She heard the clicking of her mother's purse opening and closing and then she felt a soft Kleenex under her eyes and dabbing at her cheeks. That was when she realized it wasn't rain that was making it hard to see. Her tears were the problem.

Part 4

A Very Long Weekend

Home was where Cadbury used to be but Cadbury was gone. Even though his ball was on the floor near Veronica's bed. Even though his lavender and rosemary oils were still on the side of the tub. Even though his leash was by the front door. Even though his toys were in a pile by the couch and his plaid bed was in the den next to the Scrabble set. Even though he was everywhere, he was no more.

Her mother suggested a nice bath. Veronica didn't have any better ideas so she stood in the bathroom hoping the sound of the roaring taps filling the tub would drown out her thoughts. She was handed yet another cup of tea, just the way she liked: strong and sweet and milky. Veronica drank it but she let the bath get cold. She couldn't be bothered to get undressed. She hadn't let herself cry in the vet's office. She had cried on the street but didn't feel it. She wanted to cry now, but nothing came out. She left the bathroom forgetting to drain the bathwater.

Mr. and Mrs. Morgan were lying together on the couch, her mother's head resting on her father's chest. When they heard Veronica come in they sat up and her mother dabbed her eyes. This was Veronica's loss and it was confusing to see them so upset.

"Should we build a shrine, would that be helpful? You could keep adding his things as we find them," her father offered.

"Would you like to keep a grief journal?" her mother suggested.

"You don't have to go to school tomorrow. We made you an appointment with Dr. Snope. Grief is something we all need help with. Hard to process on your own," her father said.

Veronica loved her parents more than any other people in the world, which was why she couldn't tell them that she wished she had never been born, that they had never gotten her a dog. She couldn't tell them that the sight of them sitting on the couch, drinking their wine, made her sick. She wished she could tell them to be quiet. For the love of God, just be quiet.

The next day she saw Dr. Snope. But the only part of the visit that stuck in her head was the way central casting seemed to have populated the streets of New York City with dogs. Little dogs, big dogs, dogs that had long ears like Cadbury, dogs circling trees, dogs loping alongside their owners, noses to the ground sniffing, dogs pulling their owners, owners yanking on leashes trying to pull their dogs, dogs looking up with soulful eyes at their owners. Dogs. Wonderful and loving and loyal. Man's best friend. Dogs were everywhere.

And there was Cadbury! He jumped and licked her legs and her hands. Veronica threw out her arms and pulled him toward her. He smelled like corn chips and toast and his tongue was warm and almost dry as he licked her face. But it wasn't Cadbury. It was just another beagle. A beagle just like Cadbury except that he was alive.

Her Cat Died

Cadbury died in the middle of January, five and a half weeks after he was diagnosed by Dr. Harskirey. Between her parents' concern and Dr. Snope's questioning, Veronica might as well have been placed under a microscope for observation. For a girl who liked to be invisible under ordinary circumstances, being scrutinized like this, under extraordinary circumstances, was torture.

Mary tried to be casual about her furtive attention paying, but even she was getting on Veronica's nerves. Everyone wanted Veronica to be okay because they loved her and couldn't bear to see her suffer. It was a vicious cycle. She was not okay, they wanted her to be, she felt worse for making them worry, and so it went.

Hopefully Randolf would distract her. She climbed the marble staircase Tuesday morning as Sarah-Lisa Carver, Athena Mindendorfer, Darcy Brown, Auden Georges, and everyone's new best friend, Melody Jenkins, looked over the railing. Veronica felt like a laboratory animal.

"Look. There's Veronica," she heard Melody say.

"Why are we staring at her?" Darcy asked.

"Her cat died," Auden Georges said.

"She didn't have a cat," Athena said.

Ms. Padgett came out of the classroom and ushered the girls inside. When Veronica reached the top of the stairs, Ms. Padgett hugged her. It was all Veronica could imagine wanting. But Ms. Padgett's embrace made grief burn behind her eyelids. Veronica felt naked and out of control.

She entered the classroom, keeping her head down. When she sat, Ms. Padgett led the room in Morning Verse.

I look upon the universe so tall,
The sun warms my heart and the moon guides
my soul.
The stars above sparkle and the earth below
informs my feet.

The beast and the pebble, the rain and the dawn,
Side by side.
Harmony to all things, great and small.

The sound of Morning Verse was like the voice of an old friend.

But the rest of the day wouldn't be so easy. Without a script, Veronica didn't know if she'd be able to speak or what she would say.

When Ms. Padgett was going over homework, Veronica raised her hand to ask permission to go to the bathroom.

She hid in the very last stall and cried. She took time out of math, poetry, and French to cry in there too. She even cried during the times she was in the bathroom because she had to go to the bathroom. She cried silently and she cried noisily. Sometimes she cried and instead of feeling sad, she felt wonder about the human body, her body in particular. How could it produce so many tears? She cried because her body knew no other way. *Surely I have no more tears left*, she thought over and over. But she did.

At dinner she pushed her food around. "Eat something," her mother said. Mrs. Morgan spooned rice on her daughter's plate.

"Please try," her father said.

"It will make you feel better," her mother said. "I mean, of course it isn't going to literally make you feel better . . ."

"What your mother means, dear, is that you have to eat because grieving takes a lot of energy and you have to keep up your strength."

"I think that is what *you* meant, Marvin," her mother snapped. "I am perfectly capable of speaking for myself and enjoy doing so, in fact. Must you constantly interpret for me?"

"Marion, I'm sorry, I simply was trying—"

"Marvin, you are aware that I function each and every day without you there, by my side, interpreting and helping and explaining?"

Her parents bickered until they seemed to remember Veronica was there. Then they spoke at once, apologizing over each other.

"You poor, poor girl," her father said.

"Tomorrow will be a month since he's been gone," her mother said. "That is a milestone. We care so much about all you're feeling."

"We care so much, darling."

Veronica was glad they cared. If only they could make her feel better.

The Mourner's Kaddish

Teachers didn't seem to care how much time she spent in the bathroom. They almost acted as if they thought it was a good idea. She sat on the toilet lid with her feet up so no one could see her. Voices she didn't recognize joked during math. After lunch she heard the unmistakable voice of one she did.

"My grandmother died and I didn't even cry," Sarah-Lisa said.

Veronica squeezed her knees tight and froze.

"Why is she crying all the time about an animal? My grandmother was a person and my mother told me not to cry. She said it would make people feel sorry for me."

Mr. and Mrs. Morgan told her to expect this kind of reaction from people, but it was still hurtful. "We live in a culture unable to process grief," her parents warned. "People respond by shutting down or by running away, as though death were something contagious. You really will learn from this experience, Veronica. It will make you wiser." Whatever there was to learn from heartache wasn't anything worth knowing. She would rather stay dumb.

"You were very brave, Sarah-Lisa, when your grandmother died. Very brave," Athena said. She and Sarah-Lisa must have been standing in front of the mirror combing their hair and applying lip gloss and checking their teeth. Someone else entered the bathroom. Veronica recognized Darcy's shoes under the door. Becky's shoes followed a moment later.

"Are you talking about Veronica?" Becky asked. "She sure is a sad sack. Was it her grandmother?"

"It was her dog. And I don't see what the big deal is, at all," Sarah-Lisa said. "Plus, what she did to Melody was awful!"

"What did she do to Melody?"

"She made Melody put her name on the Impressionist project," Sarah-Lisa declared.

"Poor Melody," Becky said.

"Yeah, that wasn't so nice," Darcy said.

There it was. No one wanted her. Fine with her because she had nothing to say to anyone unless it was on the subject of misery. Her knowledge on that subject was unprecedented. She could wipe the floor with all of them. Soon she'd be reading her way through lunch like Sylvie. Too bad they couldn't be loners together.

Shiva

It seemed perfectly natural to take a kitchen knife and cut her Randolf blouse that night. So she did.

"What are you doing!" her mother yelled, letting the dishwasher slam shut.

"I am sitting shiva, for Cadbury," Veronica said. She pulled at the little incision she'd made. It created a long rip. She put the knife back in the drawer and admired her newly torn blouse.

Veronica's grandfather had died when she was five. Her grandmother had ripped her dress to symbolize her torn heart. Her grandmother sat in a hard wooden chair to symbolize her pain. The mirrors in her grandmother's house were covered too, symbolizing the uselessness of vanity in the face of tragedy. For seven days Veronica watched her grandmother wear the same torn dress and sit on the same hard chair. According to her mother, she didn't brush her hair or shower the whole time. Morning and evening ten men gathered in the living room to form a minyan. They wore black coats, and their bodies rocked as their voices rhythmically whispered the mourner's kaddish: *Yisgadal v'yiskadash sh'may rabah.* The women were allowed to join in and say Amen. Veronica had no idea what the words meant, but by the second day the prayer held her like a womb.

She had been fascinated by how her grandmother gave herself to her grief. She was also deeply moved by the community of men and women who showed up every day. The women brought food and sat with her grandmother telling stories. Sometimes they made her grandmother laugh. Sometimes they cried with her. Sometimes they just sat there and didn't say a thing.

When her parents sat shiva for her grandmother it lasted only three days. The only mirror in the house that was covered was the one in the front hall. And her mother said the prayer alone. There was no minyan of ten men. Veronica felt gypped. No one sat for days telling stories and very few brought homemade food.

She had never known what the prayer meant, but when the words tumbled out of her mouth this evening, her body understood them. *Yisgadal v'yiskadash sh'may rabah . . .* Her grandmother had clung to those words as though her life depended on them and Veronica did the same. *Oseh shalom bimromav, hu ya'aseh shalom alaynu, v'al kol yisra'el, v'imru amen.*

* * *

She kept her own company in her shiva. She gathered her books on her way to bed. She passed her mother, who was sitting on the couch sorting mail.

"Veronica," Mrs. Morgan said. "I want you to take a shower. You have to take care of yourself. Daddy and I are worried."

There was no wooden furniture in the living room or Veronica would have sat down.

"Something came for you," her mother said. She handed Veronica a square red envelope.

She recognized Sarah-Lisa's slanty handwriting immediately.

"Well then, open it," her mother said. Veronica slid her finger under the flap and pulled out a pink card. There must have been a mistake. It was an invitation to Sarah-Lisa's Valentine's Day party.

She didn't understand why she had been invited to Sarah-Lisa's Valentine's Day party and then she remembered something Melody had said early on. Randolf was inclusive. Everyone was invited to everything.

"What is it, honey?"

"An invitation."

The next day after school, Mary handed Veronica more mail. This time a package. Under the brown paper were many layers of bubble wrap and tape. Whatever it was had been wrapped like something very precious. She peeled back the last layer and opened the cardboard box and in a nest of white tissue paper discovered the wooden box that contained Cadbury's ashes. She held it next to her heart. She didn't ever want to let it out of her hands.

"Yeah, but I think it's best if you put it down somewhere," Mary said. "You will be upset if you drop it and it spills."

Veronica decided to put the ashes on her nightstand next to Cadbury's collar. Mary approved.

"This came too," Mary said. She handed Veronica another package, much smaller and even more carefully wrapped than the first. This one required scissors. When everything was peeled away, Veronica discovered a sculpted silver rose wrapped around a small glass vial.

There was a note from Esme.

Dear Veronica,

I want you to know that you were the very best owner Cadbury could ever have had. I know your time together was too short but you couldn't have made him feel more loved had he lived to be a hundred. I bought you this necklace so you could put some of his ashes inside if you want to. That way he can be close to your heart at all times. I am sorry for your loss, Veronica. It is gigantic. Maybe this story will help. It helped me.

Yours,
Esme

On a separate page Esme had enclosed:

When a special animal dies, that animal goes to a place that is covered with meadows and dotted with pretty flowers. Animals run and play all day. They always have enough food and water and every animal that was old, ill, injured, or maimed is restored to optimal health. This place is called Rainbow Bridge and it is wonderful. The animals have a nearly perfect life in Rainbow Bridge except that they miss someone who had to be left behind. One day an animal looks into the distance with bright eyes. He stops running. His ears prick. He leaves the group he was playing with and flies over the green grass, his legs carrying him faster and faster. You have been spotted, and when you and your special friend finally meet, you cling together. You look once more into the trusting eyes of your pet, so long gone from your life but never replaced in your heart. You reunite knowing you will never be separated again.

The necklace came with a funnel and a tiny scoop. Veronica went right to work. Moments later, Cadbury was inside the necklace, around her neck. He was close to her heart. She put the box back on the table by her bed.

She did shower. But she wore her torn uniform and her necklace to school the next day.

To Care or Not to Care

Wearing a torn blouse was against uniform regulations, but since she was persona non grata, Veronica didn't think anyone would notice. She felt good in the wooden chair. Every room except the science lab, which had stools, had hard-backed wooden chairs. It was a mourner's delight.

"Veronica," Sarah-Lisa said, "you should run home at lunch and put on a new shirt. It's, like, ripped."

"It's torn on purpose," Veronica said. "I'm sitting shiva for my dog."

"What is that supposed to mean?" Sarah-Lisa said.

"I am in a period of mourning."

Sarah-Lisa looked at Veronica like she was speaking in tongues. Veronica pressed her back against the slats of her wooden chair feeling almost saintly, like a monk wearing a hair shirt.

Later, in art, Sylvie and Veronica were at the sink, washing paintbrushes. The water was warm and the soap felt soft against the bristles. Sylvie noticed Veronica's necklace.

"It's filled with ashes," Veronica told her.

"Nice," Sylvie said with a genuine smile. Veronica had expected Sylvie to flinch. But she didn't.

At lunch, Athena put her tray down next to Veronica's. Athena pushed her school lunch around while Veronica unpacked her cheddar cheese sandwich. Her mother had also put in a Tupperware of peeled pomegranate. The seeds glistened like jewels. Veronica ate a handful.

"I've never seen a necklace like that," Athena said. Veronica moved closer and let Athena hold it. "Is it an antique?" she asked.

"No. It comes from a crematorium," Sylvie said, piping in from out of nowhere as she so often did.

Veronica held the vial up to the light.

Melody and Sarah-Lisa walked over. Since Veronica's outing as the person who was mean to Melody, Sarah-Lisa had taken Melody on like a charity case. Maybe all the A Team's social atoms could rebond, allowing Athena and Veronica to attach while Sarah-Lisa and Melody could form a new and separate chemical chain.

"What's a crematorium?" Sarah-Lisa asked.

"It's where the remains of dead bodies are burned," Athena said.

How did Athena know things like that? She wasn't one of those people whose heads were filled with useless facts so she could show off. She was just a person with too much life experience.

"My dog, the one that died, that you met, is in there. Some of him."

"Oh my gosh," Melody gasped.

Veronica couldn't tell if Melody was scared or fascinated by the necklace, or both.

"Her dog's ashes are in there?" Sarah-Lisa asked incredulously.

"Yes, they are," Veronica said. She looked right at Sarah-Lisa.

"Let me see that," Sarah-Lisa said. But she wouldn't look at Veronica. She looked at the necklace. She put the vial in her hand. "There is no way her dog is in there."

"He is," Veronica declared. Disturbing Sarah-Lisa with this information filled Veronica with a joyous sensation. "I mean, not all of him, but some of him," Veronica added for good measure.

"It's touching," Athena said.

"It's not touching," Sarah-Lisa said, but she was still holding the necklace in her hand. "It's disgusting."

"It is sort of disgusting," Melody said, moving closer to Sarah-Lisa.

"I'm sorry, but I can't sit here with dead dog matter.

Not during lunch," Sarah-Lisa said, and let go of the necklace. She picked up her tray and left. Melody followed.

"I think it's interesting. To care that much," Athena said. She smiled at Veronica before walking away to join Sarah-Lisa and Melody. Veronica watched them go, wondering if she would ever feel comfortable with them again.

"It's not interesting to care that much," Sylvie said to Veronica when everyone was gone. "It's necessary."

Athena was waiting at Veronica's locker after French. She was standing so close, Veronica could practically count her eyelashes.

"Athena?" Veronica asked.

"Yes," Athena said.

Veronica wanted to ask what she'd always wanted to ask: Why aren't we best friends? But she sensed Sarah-Lisa coming around the corner any second and that was the answer to her question anyway. They weren't best friends because Sarah-Lisa got there first.

"You should really come to Sarah-Lisa's Valentine's party. You haven't come to one yet," Athena said. "Sometimes parties cheer people up."

"Maybe," Veronica said.

"There are always strawberries the size of human fists there. And a chocolate fountain. You should really come."

Sarah-Lisa rounded the lockers and Veronica felt like she and Athena had been caught. Doing what? Talking? Sarah-Lisa always made Veronica feel bad about something.

"Athena. Come," Sarah-Lisa said. Athena stood between Veronica and Sarah-Lisa. Then she followed Sarah-Lisa down the hall like a good little doggie.

Far Enough

Ms. Padgett handed out progress reports at the end of the day. Veronica's came with a letter, which she doubted was talking about her wonderful contributions to class. Her parents weren't idiots—they had to know things weren't going well. But she wasn't looking forward to the discussion her parents were likely to engage her in after reading the letter. She came home and put the letter and the report under the flour jar on the kitchen counter. Maybe no one would see it.

"What is this?" asked her father, holding up the letter. When you wanted him to notice things he saw nothing. But now, of course, his eyes were radar.

Veronica was trying to think of ways to stall the inevitable. She didn't want to watch her parents' faces express disappointment.

The buzzer from the intercom rang and saved her. There was a mad rush to set the table. Veronica and her father gathered plates and silverware while Marion Morgan dug in her purse frantically for her wallet. Everyone was so distracted Veronica actually thought she might get away without answering the original question.

"What the hell is this?" Marvin Morgan asked again.

Veronica felt a headache coming. Why didn't he just open the envelope already?

"Burritos," his wife declared. She took the envelope out of his hand.

"Burritos, oh boy!" he said. "Which one is mine?"

"They're all the same, veggie. It's meatless Monday in the Morgan house. Pass the pico de gallo, please, and the sour cream."

"Marion?"

"Marvin?"

"It's Friday."

"That is true, dear heart, but I forgot on Monday." Her mother opened the envelope.

Veronica winced. Her mother read it slowly and handed it to her father. "We expected your grades to take a bit of a beating," her mother said. "But this business with Melody, that is not good. That is not something only limited to you. You took advantage of that girl and it seems like something that needs discussing."

"I didn't take advantage of her. She handed in work with my name on it, but I never asked her to," Veronica said.

"This is yummy, by the way," Marvin said, devouring his burrito.

"Marvin."

"What?"

"Please. Let Veronica talk."

Veronica didn't want to reenter the fishbowl of her parents' concern. She thought they were going to let Dr. Snope do his work and leave her alone. How did she feel about disappointing Ms. Padgett and basically lying about doing work on a project she had not done work on? She felt distinctly not good about it. But how could she have chosen schoolwork over spending time with Cadbury every second while she still had the chance? She still missed him and no matter what she tried to fill herself with—Scrabble games with Mary or cuddling with her mom—everything just trickled out and she was empty all over again.

"I am grieving," Veronica finally said because it was true and because she hoped it would end the discussion. "And," she added, "I agree with Daddy, this burrito is good."

"That's my girl!" her father said. There was nothing like discussing food to get the whole Morgan family off on a tangent. Veronica could probably murder someone but they would still enjoy talking about a new place to get take-out.

"It's that new place on Ninety-Ninth," her mother added. "The fish tacos are supposed to be good too."

"Maybe we can have those on Monday. Fish doesn't have meat in it," Marvin said.

Whatever hope Veronica had of changing the subject, or at least the dynamic in the room, disappeared because Marion Morgan looked at her husband like a child who had done something wrong. "I'm just saying," he added sheepishly. Meanwhile, the child who was supposed to speak said nothing.

"Honey," her mother said, "you are grieving. And you are doing a beautiful job, but Daddy, Dr. Snope, and apparently Ms. Padgett, and I, for that matter, feel that you have perhaps retreated as far as is healthy. Right, Marvin?"

"Yes," Marvin replied.

"Would you care to elaborate?" his wife asked.

"No. I think you are doing a wonderful job. Pass the guacawhosie, please."

"Veronica, maybe it's time to make some steps toward rejoining your life."

Veronica woke up every day. She went to school. She was doing what was required. What more could they ask of her?

"You were starting to make friends. Friends can help you. It's not good to wallow. You were invited to that Valentine's party. Right?"

"Yes," Veronica said.

"We think you should go."

"You told me to take my time!" Veronica said, genuinely dismayed.

"Marvin," Marion Morgan pleaded.

"Yes," Marvin said.

"Help me."

My poor mother, Veronica thought.

"Your mother thinks you should go to the Sarah-Lisa party," her father said.

"So do you," her mother added.

"So do I . . ."

"So does Ms. Padgett. Sweetheart, it has been many weeks since we lost Cadbury."

"Would you like to finish, darling?" Marvin Morgan said pointedly. "You asked me to take over but you continue to interrupt. Perhaps you would be most comfortable if I stopped talking."

Marion Morgan put her burrito down and excused herself from the table. Discussions between her parents devolving into arguments were becoming commonplace. Marvin Morgan appeared to be caught between the urge to follow his wife and the instinct to stay with his daughter.

"Sweetheart," he said. "We love you. And we want you to find some kind of balance between your mourning and the life that is very much right in front of you. Ms. Padgett feels it is important for you to accept the gestures of friendship the girls in your community are making. We want you to go to that girl's party."

"Honey, just try," her mother said from the hall. "If it truly is unbearable we won't stay long. But I think it is time to begin the process of normalization. Just act as if. Sometimes if you can't do it, you fake it and eventually your feelings and your actions catch up with each other."

"But—" Veronica started to explain. She didn't bother to finish though because the discussion was clearly over.

Black and White

Marion Morgan was Veronica's escort to the party at Sarah-Lisa's. That had to be a little better than Marvin coming too and eating too many appetizers and speaking too loudly. But Veronica still dreaded getting out of the elevator. Sarah-Lisa lived in the kind of apartment that had its own elevator. When the door opened, she and her mother were already inside the Carver apartment.

"Take a look at this, would you!" Mrs. Morgan exclaimed. "Isn't this something? We are just in the foyer, and it is already unbelievable!"

Veronica stood next to her mother, feeling like a line drawing someone had taken an eraser to. She was smudgy, unsure, undefined.

A maid dressed in a black uniform with a white apron scurried over. She took their coats and directed them to the living room at the end of a long hall. Everything everywhere was white: the walls, the floors, most of the furniture. If Mrs. Carver hadn't come barreling down the hall toward them, Veronica thought they would have most likely gotten lost, the way people with snow blindness become hopelessly disoriented amid miles and miles of snow.

"Welcome!" Mrs. Carver said. "Come in. Come in!" Veronica assumed Mrs. Carver was mixing them up with some other guests because there was no reason for her to be happy to see them or, for that matter, to even know who they were.

"I am so glad you could join us," Sarah-Lisa's mother said, ushering them into a big room filled with more white furniture and unfamiliar people. "You are the mysterious new girl we've all been dying to meet. Sarah-Lisa had a wonderful time trick-or-treating with you and then you just disappeared. Went right off the radar."

She seemed genuine and nice. Maybe Sarah-Lisa was adopted. That would explain a lot of things.

A waiter came by with a tray of champagne and another brought skewers of something grilled and arranged on giant leaves.

"All the girls are waiting for you in Sarah-Lisa's lair. I would have thought they would be gathered around the chocolate, but it just goes to show you what I know," Sarah-Lisa's mother said, munching a skewer. "Why don't you go find them and let me chat with your mother."

Mrs. Carver was wearing a white dress that looked like

a toga. It was held up on one shoulder by a gigantic brooch in the shape of a kite. Usually larger-than-life people made Veronica uncomfortable, but there was something appealing about Mrs. Carver.

"I just love what you've done with the space, Mrs. Carver," Veronica's mother said. Veronica chewed quietly on a mystery kabob.

"Please. Call me Peggy," Sarah-Lisa's mother said. "Mrs. Carver is my mother-in-law!" She howled at her own joke and Veronica thought the pictures might fall off the walls. "That is so cliché, I know," Peggy said, "but it is honestly how I *feel.* I don't ever want to be Mrs. Carver. I will forever be Peggy Lehman. I never change my name. Not any of the times I get married. Do you change yours? Not that I think there is anything wrong with it."

There was a black-and-white photograph behind Mrs. Lehman-Carver (whatever her name was) of a girl, about Veronica's age, playing naked in the woods. The photograph was compelling, like Mrs. Lehman-Carver, even though Veronica didn't exactly like it.

"I did change my name," Veronica's mother said. She helped herself to a glass of champagne. "I'm a professional woman but I love having my magazine subscriptions refer to me as Mrs. Marvin Morgan."

"Ohhhh. It's almost kitschy. I love it!" Sarah-Lisa's mother said, laughing.

Veronica's mother could go anywhere and have something to say. Was it a skill or a personality disorder? Veronica wondered.

Another waiter, carrying a block of ice with oysters artfully nestled in little crevices atop it, stopped next to Mrs. Morgan. Veronica could smell the briny sea and she had to turn away as her mother sucked one of the jiggly things out of its shell deep into her mouth.

"Go," her mother whispered in her ear as their host said hello to another guest. "The sooner you say hello to the girls, the sooner we can leave." Veronica decided this was probably the only good advice she had gotten from her mother in a while. She detached herself from her mother's arm while Sarah-Lisa's mother explained, "We had to buy apartments on different floors just to get the ceiling height right. I can't bear low ceilings! Can you?"

Veronica climbed the white stairs in her black dress. The Carver house was supernaturally clean, carpets and all. They must have a team of cleaning specialists working around the clock, seven days a week. Veronica felt like a walking stain.

At the top of the stairs, she opened a door revealing a second living room with a big TV, and three couches, and a bar. No one was there so she kept going. The next door she walked through led to a bedroom. In the middle of a king-size bed, a terrier of some kind rested on a poufy dog pillow. It might have been a Jack Russell. The animal stirred and looked up at Veronica, yawning and stretching before going back to sleep. She was about to go pat the dog when she felt a hand on her shoulder.

"You're here," Athena said. "There was a lot of discussion about you. I thought you'd come, but no one else did. Come on, we're in Peggy's closet."

Veronica abandoned the sweet dog and followed Athena. Athena had that power still. "Sarah-Lisa will be so surprised you're here. I can't imagine what you must think, being here for the first time. This house is like a hundred times bigger than anyone else's house. Isn't it?"

"How many living rooms do they have?" Veronica asked.

"According to her family, the room downstairs is the only living room. The one up here is the theater. Look, they even have a popcorn maker. It was so fun when we watched *Grease*. Remember? Oh right, you weren't here."

Sarah-Lisa's mother's closet was so big it was quite possible they had joined several apartments to make it, as well. Mrs. Lehman-Carver had about two hundred fifty pairs of shoes, at least two hundred pairs of boots, dozens of hats and coats, and hundreds of sweaters, all arranged by color. The girls were busy trying things on and admiring themselves in the mirror.

"Look who I found," Athena said, holding Veronica's hand and pulling her inside.

If Athena stayed with her, being at the party wouldn't be so bad. It might even be fun.

"Hi, Veronica," Melody said. It was nice to see Melody outside of school, in a different context. Maybe tonight could repair what had gone wrong.

Veronica looked around and saw Sylvie. It must be true that everyone was invited if both she and Sylvie were there. Coco Weitzner was wincing in a particularly painful-looking pair of high heels and smiling in the mirror.

"Do these look good with this dress?" Coco asked. Veronica thought they did and almost said so, but she was so happy being under Athena's care and didn't want to draw attention to it. Sarah-Lisa might notice and take Athena back.

"Who wants to go first?" Sarah-Lisa said.

"Do we have to play Truth or Dare?" Melody said.

"Yeah, Melody, we do. We always play Truth or Dare," Becky said.

"It's true. And I dare us not to," Sylvie said. Everyone looked at her like she was crazy.

"Yes, Melody, we always do. But if you're scared of a dare just tell the truth. No biggie," Athena said. She turned and winked at Veronica. Veronica loved this vantage point, standing safely holding hands with Athena. It was like being on top of a mountain where the air was better. She never wanted to come down.

"Okay. Here we go," Sarah-Lisa said. "Melody. Truth or dare?"

"Well, it depends."

"On what the dare is? That's not fair," Auden Georges said.

"Okay. Truth?" Melody said in her Melody sort of way.

"Is that a question, Melody? Or a statement?" Sarah-Lisa asked.

"A statement?" Melody said.

"Okay. Truth. Melody Jenkins: Have you ever seen a boy naked?"

Peals of laughter came from every corner of the closet and Melody's face turned the color of a red rubber gym ball. Poor Melody.

Veronica dreaded what they would ask her. Probably something terrible like whether or not she had her period yet, at which point she would die.

"Oh my gosh. That is so rude," Melody said. She hid her head in her hands. "No! I haven't!"

"Can I try on your mother's Chanel?" Maggie Fogel asked.

"Go for it," Sarah-Lisa said. "Darcy Brown, your turn. Truth or dare?"

"Um . . . dare," Darcy said.

Sarah-Lisa's face lit up like a forest fire. "Yay! Someone's got guts!" she said. She called Athena over to help her with the question. Sarah-Lisa and her best friend plotted in whispers.

Veronica was nervous even though she wasn't the one being dared. She was not volunteering ever. They better not ask her.

"Okeydoke, Darcy Brown," Sarah-Lisa said to her newest victim. "Your dare is to go downstairs and pile the smallest plate with the biggest amount of yummy refreshments."

"Liquids *and* solids—" Athena interjected.

"Yes—liquids and solids, and bring them up here. In thirty seconds. Ready? Go!"

Just thinking about all that white furniture and white carpeting made Veronica scared. She worried for Darcy.

"Veronica. Are you going to join in or just spy on us?" Sarah-Lisa asked.

"I'm not spying," Veronica said. Although she was standing on the side, watching and not participating. From their perspective it must have looked like she was spying.

"Maggie, you're such a slob. You left my mother's favorite skirt on the floor," Sarah-Lisa scolded.

"Sorry."

"Well, hang it up," Sarah-Lisa declared.

"Why don't we dress you up, Veronica? You look too somber in black. This is a party. What should we dress Veronica in, you guys?" Athena said.

"What's wrong with black?" Sylvie asked. "It's my favorite color."

"Exactly," Athena said to Sylvie. "I mean, you are not exactly known for your lighthearted goofiness."

Athena walked back to Veronica and sized her up from every angle. Auden Georges held up a pair of knee-high brown boots with appliquéd shapes and flowers sewn onto them. Athena approved. Becky Shickler unfolded a giant lace scarf and held it against Veronica's face as if she were matching fabric swatches with paint chips and tile samples. Athena took Veronica by the hand and led her to the fur section of the closet. Athena ran her hand along a row of Sarah-Lisa's mother's coats and finally settled on a short hooded jacket of some kind of white fur.

"Wait! I was going to wear that," Sarah-Lisa said.

"Oh, S-L. Be nice. You can come in here any day and wear whatever you want. Look how cute it is on her!" It was like a dream come true, being defended against Sarah-Lisa by Athena. Veronica was beside herself.

"You look like an old-fashioned skater in Central Park! Give her the muff!" Auden Georges said.

Veronica looked at herself in the mirror, but all she could see were Sarah-Lisa's eyes, staring at her from behind like two black darts. They were pointing right at her and they looked like they could hurt.

The sweet little terrier wandered in and sniffed around.

Veronica gave him her hand, which he licked gently before walking to the other side of the closet.

"He has such expensive taste!" Coco said, laughing. The dog had a black Prada purse in his mouth.

"Binky, *no*!" Sarah-Lisa yelled. "Don't eat that! Oh my gosh, Binky! You're so dumb. My mother is going to kill me."

Esme always said that a dog is only as dumb as his owner. Sarah-Lisa obviously didn't know that.

"Veronica, naturally we only see you at school in your uniform, but do you always wear black when you aren't at school?" Auden asked.

"It makes you seem sad," Melody said.

"It's because her cat died," Coco said.

"She didn't have a cat, she had a dog," Athena said. Binky dropped the purse and went deeper into the closet.

"Uh-oh, he's going after the Chanel skirt," Sylvie said. Binky, being a terrier, was a very good jumper. He was three feet off the ground, determined to make contact with the skirt and pull it from its hanger. He got it in his mouth. Sarah-Lisa took hold of the hanger and a tug of war began. The dog refused to let go.

"Careful," Athena said.

"Binky, *no*!" Sarah-Lisa said, pulling at the fabric while Binky clamped down tighter. Veronica couldn't stand the way Sarah-Lisa was hollering. Obviously Binky thought Sarah-Lisa was playing with him. His tail was wagging like crazy and he was snorting happy, laughing sounds. "Binky!" Sarah-Lisa yelled, and pulled harder.

"It's going to rip, Sarah-Lisa, stop pulling," Athena said. Sure enough, a few moments later, the skirt ripped away from the waistband and Sarah-Lisa exploded. "Binky, you idiot! I am going to get in so much trouble," she said, smacking Binky with one of her mother's shoes.

The dog whimpered and hid under a bench. Veronica was furious. She picked up the shoe Binky had been hit with and hurled it at Sarah-Lisa. "Never hurt an animal. Don't *ever* do that," Veronica told everyone.

She walked out of the closet and slammed the door with all her might. The shoe hadn't even hit Sarah-Lisa. Nothing she did made an impact.

Goodbye, and Thank You for Inviting Me

Sarah-Lisa's many apartments joined together to make one house was like a white rat maze and Veronica couldn't find her way out. She found an office, a guest room, a palatial bathroom. All she wanted to find was stairs. The stairs led to her mother. But the stairs were nowhere in sight. She turned down a hall and ended up in what had to be Sarah-Lisa's room.

Of course Sarah-Lisa had a canopy bed. She had everything. She even had a dog she didn't deserve.

She took in Sarah-Lisa Carver's well-organized vanity with its mirror and its lip glosses and fancy brush set and the matching nail scissor and emery board. Sarah-Lisa had a cloth-covered bulletin board covered in notes from Athena—*Dear S-L, C U after school xoxox*—and so many pictures of the two of them having so much fun.

Sarah-Lisa's dresser was right next to the vanity and had

a perfect glass animal collection and a tower of powder blue boxes from Tiffany proudly displayed on top. Veronica opened Sarah-Lisa's drawers. All her cashmere cardigans were inside, folded perfectly and arranged by color, just like the clothes in Mrs. Carver's closet.

She put a navy blue one next to her face. It was soft and smelled like it had been washed in expensive perfume. Veronica took it to the vanity, carefully laid it over the mirror, and cut off all the pearl buttons. She went back to the dresser and took out a pale blue cardigan. She cut its arms off. She cut holes in the armpits of an ivory one. One by one, she destroyed all of Sarah-Lisa Carver's cashmere cardigans.

When she was finished she put the scissors back on the vanity and was overtaken by the strangest sensation. She'd left her body. She was there, but she wasn't there. She was at a distance, watching herself in the bedroom of a fancy girl named Sarah-Lisa Carver. She needed to find the hall that led downstairs. She would find her mother and they would go home. Oh, to be home, to have a few days without having to see any of those girls. She wanted her mother but came face-to-face with Athena Mindendorfer instead. Her blood stopped moving through her body. It coagulated like Jell-O.

"Veronica! What are you doing?" Athena asked.

Veronica couldn't answer the question. She'd messed up all of Sarah-Lisa's pretty sweaters. But she hadn't planned it. She couldn't explain anything. She walked out of Sarah-Lisa's room, away from the damage and away from Athena, who would never choose her over Sarah-Lisa. She was in her altered state of being. Detached. A spectator. Her life wasn't her own. What happened here tonight was scenes from a scary movie of a life that belonged to someone else. She didn't need to be afraid.

She escorted her disembodied self down the stairs, which had suddenly appeared before her. She wished she'd thought to do this earlier; leave her body, be here by not really being here. It solved so many problems.

Sarah-Lisa came down the stairs behind her, holding half of the desecrated pale blue cashmere cardigan, followed by an army of hysterical girls. There was shouting, and in the midst of a huge commotion, which should have shaken her to the core, she felt very little. The real Veronica was somewhere else, safe and sound, protected by her numbness.

Sarah-Lisa waved her cashmere remnants in Veronica's face and Sarah-Lisa's mother shook her and stripped off her white fur jacket.

She thought she heard her mother tell her to say, "Thank you for inviting me," so she did. She thought she heard Sarah-Lisa's mother telling Mrs. Morgan that her daughter needed a psychiatrist and Mrs. Morgan saying something like, "Thank you very much, she has one. Plus two as parents. One plus two equals three. Good night."

The Center of Another Bed

That night, Veronica lay in the center of her parents' bed half-asleep. Her parents were holed up in their bathroom. Veronica could hear every word.

"Well, she certainly is grieving," Mr. Morgan said after hearing his wife explain what had happened at the party he did not attend.

"But what are we going to do?" Mrs. Morgan said, whispering. "We have to do something."

"I think she needs to talk more about processing her feelings. For a start."

"She doesn't want to," Mrs. Morgan said. "We ask her constantly to process. She won't."

"Tough," Mr. Morgan said. "And she is going to have to apologize to that girl."

"But I thought she was grieving so wonderfully. I thought she was doing so well. She acted out at school by not doing that project. She had his ashes, the letter from Esme, she sat a shiva . . ."

"She just needs some help, Marion. Her teacher told us as much. We obviously are not helping her."

"No, we're not," Mrs. Morgan said, and burst into tears.

Fake It Till You Make It

Veronica spent the night in her parents' bed.

The next morning she was brought a cup of tea and a pad of paper. She had instructions to compose letters to both Mrs. Lehman-Carver and to Sarah-Lisa.

She looked at the blank paper, having no idea what to say. Her parents suggested she begin with "I'm sorry." And as if that was enough help, they both left the room.

Veronica struggled. The paper was blank and she couldn't imagine filling it with words. Or with ideas. Her handwriting was so undeveloped compared with Sarah-Lisa's. She decided to pretend she was someone else. A person who possessed more integrity, a person who could actually write a meaningful letter.

Dear Sarah-Lisa,

Thank you for inviting me to your party. I was not a very good citizen and I should not have cut all your beautiful sweaters. I am sorry. I was wrong. I am sorry that since I have not come to any of your other parties, this is the party you will remember me by. I love animals very much and I miss my dog. I lost my temper. I am sorry. I don't expect you to forgive me. But I cannot forgive myself unless I apologize to you.

I am very sorry.

Truly,
Veronica

Mrs. Morgan walked in with a breakfast tray and presented Veronica with pancakes and juice.

"You need to keep up your strength," she said. "How is the letter coming?" Veronica handed her mother what she'd written. Mrs. Morgan read it over.

"Excellent," she said. Veronica put syrup on her pancakes and took a bite. "Now another letter, to her mother."

Veronica's soul had more squeezing to do. Ugh. Mrs. Lehman.

"Fake it till you make it," her mother said, and left the room. Veronica ate the pancakes and drank her juice. The letter to Mrs. Lehman was a little easier because she didn't know her.

Dear Mrs. Lehman,

Your daughter has the most beautiful things in one room I have ever seen. I am so sorry that I was jealous.

I will work out something with my parents and pay to replace all the sweaters I ruined. Please send us a bill. I am so sorry I ruined your evening with my behavior.

I am sincerely more sorry and ashamed than you will ever know.

Sincerely,
Veronica Louise Morgan

Veronica put the breakfast tray on the floor and went to sleep.

In the afternoon her mother came in. "Put your coat on," she said. "We are going for a walk. Daddy too."

Veronica got out of bed and got dressed. She put on her coat and scarf in a daze and stood dutifully next to her parents. Mr. Morgan and Mrs. Morgan took hold of their daughter, one on either side, and supported her as they walked out of the apartment, in and out of the elevator, and onto the street.

"When I was a child," Mrs. Morgan said, "the whole community came on the seventh day of a shiva and walked the grieving family around the block. Daddy and I want to be your community. We thought we were doing enough. But we haven't been."

When Veronica was very little her parents used to walk with her like this, one on either side. On the count of three they would lift her in the air. She would make them do it again and again.

"Honey," her father said, "you loved that dog. And you were so good to that dog. You took such amazing care of that dog. We are proud of you."

"We sure are, Veronica. You have an incredible heart."

The Morgan family walked along Fifth Avenue past the hospital, down 102nd Street with its funny brownstones mixed in with big apartment buildings and north on Madison Avenue past the bagel store and west on 103rd Street until they were headed south on Fifth. When they ended up back at their apartment Veronica let them lift her over the threshold.

The Parting of the Red Sea

Veronica unpeeled two stamps and stuck them very carefully on the top right-hand corners of the envelopes containing her apology letters. It was very important to her that each stamp line up with the corner of its envelope perfectly. When she dropped the letters in the mailbox she felt an ounce of misery slide down the chute with them.

On her way to school the next day she realized everyone probably already knew about Sarah-Lisa's party and what the girl with the overactive scissors had done there.

She imagined all the telephone calls and texts as one girl told another girl and another girl and another girl all about Veronica Morgan, the Wiccan in the sixth grade who wore her dead dog's ashes around her neck and cut all of Sarah-Lisa Carver's cashmere sweaters into little pieces.

Mrs. Harrison would ask Veronica what kind of person avoided assignments and purposely let another girl do all the work on a project designed for two. Regardless of the fact that Veronica wrote Sarah-Lisa and Sarah-Lisa's mother apologies, Mrs. Harrison would ask what kind of person would destroy another person's property. Then Mrs. Harrison would answer the question herself, kindly explaining that the kind of person Veronica apparently was was not the kind of person who belonged at Randolf. Well, getting thrown out might be better than staying. Oh God. Her anxiety was overwhelming. Sleep had been the only escape, but now she was awake.

She turned down the block to Randolf and girls who usually ran past, busy with their own lives and their own popularity, were obviously acutely aware of her.

Everyone looked at her as she walked by.

Everywhere Veronica went, the girls dispersed as if Veronica gave off a negative ionic charge. By the time Veronica got to her classroom, so many people had moved away from her she felt like Moses parting the Red Sea.

Athena whisked Sarah-Lisa out of the way as though Veronica was dangerous, as though she was going to cut them both with a pair of scissors.

If only, Veronica thought. *If only I could cut this whole school into little tiny pieces.*

At her table she unloaded her backpack trying to gauge, without looking up, who was watching her. Out of the corner of her eye she saw Sarah-Lisa. She hadn't had time to replace her sweaters. Sarah-Lisa was cardigan-less, like everyone else.

* * *

The spring science expo was in a few weeks and Mr. Bower was beside himself in anticipation. Mr. Bower didn't like to judge people on tests as much as on their creativity, so this project counted for half their overall grade and they had just three weeks to complete it. Each two-person team had to create a three-dimensional project pertaining to energy, power, or photosynthesis. Veronica's heart pounded as he explained the instructions. If Mr. Bower paired her with Sarah-Lisa she would absolutely die. Writing the letters was one thing, but spending time with Sarah-Lisa was another. Veronica was going to have to do household chores until she was forty-seven years old before she'd be able to pay her parents back for all that cashmere.

Plus, she doubted the Carver family would ever welcome her in their home or anywhere near their precious daughter, so how would she and Sarah-Lisa finish their project? Come to think of it, no one would want to work with her. What an awful thought.

"Becky Shickler," Mr. Bower said as he studied a list, "you and Tillie Allen are a pair, Liv O'Malley and Darcy Brown will work together, and Veronica Morgan, you and Sylvie Samuels will be paired."

Veronica was shocked. Sylvie? Oh my goodness. Sylvie, who had been right there and saw her try to hit Sarah-Lisa with a Prada shoe? In reality, everyone probably had had a good view. And if they didn't they got the verbal playback. Ugh. No. She couldn't work with anyone. They would all avoid her and do what she'd done to Melody with the Monet project, except they wouldn't put Veronica's name on the final project. She was going to flunk the expo and it was half her whole grade. No pressure. She couldn't wait to go home and go to sleep.

Conspiracies

That night, Veronica tried to act normal. She set the table and carried out the water pitcher. But she couldn't keep her mind off being paired with Sylvie and how she might get out of it. A partnership of any kind was the enemy. A partnership would ruin her prospects of getting back on track academically. She felt so bad about how disappointed in her Ms. Padgett must have been about the Monet project. She wanted to redeem herself somehow, and if she did well in science maybe Mr. Bower would talk to Ms. Padgett. If she could work alone, she'd have a chance to work her tail off and do a decent project.

Her hands trembled. She filled the water glasses carefully, certain she was going to flunk out of middle school. Ugh. She had to convince her parents to talk to Mr. Bower and let her do the expo project alone.

Mr. Morgan sat down at the table but got right back up.

"Where are you going?" his wife asked.

"I realized that this evening requires beer," he said. Veronica looked at her father, then her mother, trying to figure out which parent would be easier to convince that she needed to work alone. Sometimes her mother was the more understanding one, but she'd been pretty tough lately—making her go to the party and write those letters. Her father returned from the kitchen with his beer. He sat down and took a long drink. Her parents conferred with their eyes.

"Veronica, your father and I have something rather difficult we need to discuss with you," her mother said. Her father took another long drink from his beer and Veronica realized her parents were getting divorced. Why else would he need a drink? This was too much.

"Veronica lovey," her mother said between bites of falafel, "Mary is having surgery on her hip." Veronica must have looked terrified because her father jumped into the conversation as though he were rescuing her from imminent danger.

"It is not a tricky operation. Please don't worry. In fact, hip replacements are so successful and so quick they've actually given specialists a good name. Our Mary will come out intact and dancing. They can do them in their sleep. Pass the kibbe."

Both her father and her mother had a habit of comforting Veronica by chattering so much it was hard to follow what they were saying. Something about Mary and surgery and Middle Eastern food. But at least it seemed her parents were staying married.

"Here, darling," her mother said. She passed the kibbe to her husband. "No, the only problem with Mary having this operation, which will absolutely be a success, you have nothing to worry about, lovey, people twenty years older than Mary have this done and handle it brilliantly. The only problem with Mary's surgery is you. I'm not sure how you will feel about this, but you have to go to a friend's house after school for the three weeks Mary is out."

The hummus Veronica had in her mouth arrived in her gut with the force of a cinder block dropped from the roof of a ten-story building.

There was no way she could be with normal people. Her life was so abnormal now, all by her own doing, but nonetheless, she couldn't possibly spend time with someone normal. She was miserable, friendless, flunking out of school, and on top of that she had so much hummus stuck in her stomach, she was probably going to upchuck to death. Mrs. Cohen and Cricket couldn't begin to understand what she was going through.

But it turned out she was not going to Cricket Cohen's house for the three weeks Mary was recuperating.

"Sylvie?" Veronica said, spitting water all over herself. She had just taken a large gulp, hoping to dislodge the hummus, and it all came up when she heard the news. "I can't go to her house! I don't even *know* her."

It was a conspiracy. First Mr. Bower and now her parents. Where would it end? When would it end?

"Honey, you are supposed to be doing a science project together," her mother said, as though that made everything all right.

Veronica hadn't even mentioned the science project yet. How did they know?

"Ms. Padgett actually suggested it," her father interjected. Veronica wanted to scream. They had been talking about her behind her back like everyone else.

"All of us have been very concerned," her father continued. "We know you're grieving. Your emotions have been very deep."

"As they should be," her mother added.

"Certainly, as they should be. Cadbury was a terrible loss and we know you are working hard with Dr. Snope."

"We think you are doing a marvelous job, by the way," her mother said. "You are walking right along the path of grief toward the road of acceptance. There are many detours along the way, anger . . ."

"Denial," her father added. "It's not just a river in Egypt."

"Oh God!" Veronica said.

"Anger. It is natural for you to act out. It is perfect. It means you are going through the necessary steps of the grieving process. Denial, anger . . ."

"Honey, we're so proud of you."

"Please. Can we not talk about it?" Veronica begged.

"Veronica lovey, it is important that you do this science project. Even while you are completing the cycle of grief."

"What do you mean?" Veronica asked. But she knew exactly what they meant. She hadn't done the Monet project so she was being punished, put in lockup with Sylvie Samuels because no one trusted her. Oh, why hadn't she just gone to the museum with Melody? The repercussions of that decision were apparently endless. She had ruined everything.

"You need to do your science project and you need a babysitter and—"

"I'm not a baby!"

"Your mother doesn't actually mean you are a baby, she just means you shouldn't be alone every afternoon."

Alone every afternoon was exactly what Veronica wanted. Alone for the rest of her life would be even better.

"You hate me!" she said, and ran down the hall. "You hate me!" She slammed her door because at that moment Veronica hated her parents. And Sylvie. And herself. And Cadbury for dying.

Part 5

For the Love of Science

Veronica could not understand why everyone was in love with Mr. Bower, but she could not deny that her classmates acted like a bunch of first-rate ninnies around him. They fawned and giggled and whispered so much that Mr. Bower spent most of his science periods deeply saddened by his students' disinterest in scientific notions. They were only interested in his newly acquired beard and what he may or may not have done over the weekend.

The situation was ironic because if one of the girls who was in love with him enjoyed science, Mr. Bower might actually marry her. But he would never think of them as marriage material as long as they weren't able to pay attention to science. Veronica wondered if he had assigned these projects as a way of getting the girls to concentrate on each other—and maybe even science—for a few weeks, instead of on him.

"It is so handsome the way his hair sticks up on the top," Coco whispered to Darcy Brown.

"For the love of science!" Mr. Bower declared. "Will you please focus!"

Darcy Brown looked at him like she was going to melt off her stool right onto the floor.

Veronica caught Sylvie rolling her eyes right at Darcy. That was one thing about Sylvie. She really didn't care what other people thought. Sylvie was her own best friend.

Mr. Bower finally gave up trying to address the class as a whole and went around table by table, gauging the status of the projects. He had handed out sheets during the last class on which they were supposed to have jotted down ideas that interested them. All the girls probably wanted to write down his name on the sheet because he was the only thing that really interested them.

When Mr. Bower got to Veronica and Sylvie's table he asked them if they had met and talked about their ideas. The answer to that question was no. There was an awkward silence.

"Not yet," Sylvie said.

"All right, well, let me hear your ideas," Mr. Bower said.

Ideas? Veronica had no ideas at all. She had only begun to wrap her brain around the fact that she had to do the project with Sylvie in the first place. That was as far as she'd gotten. In fact the sheet of ideas they'd been given to consider as possible projects was still in her folder, unread since their last class.

"I'm interested in a project with plants," Sylvie said. "Like what if we had two plants and we treated one plant really well and gave it clean water and sunshine and plant food and the other plant was left in a closet or something?"

"That's excellent!" Mr. Bower beamed. "To speed up your results, you could go further and actually feed one plant contaminated water and repot it in bad soil." Sylvie looked thrilled. It seemed like a stupid idea to Veronica, but it was obviously an idea that she was going to participate in since she had no ideas of her own. Whatever bad fate lay in store for a plant kept in a closet, out of the light, Veronica was sure hers would be worse. At the very least they would both wilt and die.

"Veronica?" Mr. Bower asked. "I'm asking you a question."

"What?" Veronica said, startled.

"How do you feel about the contamination idea? I don't want to interfere with your vision," Mr. Bower said.

"Fine," Veronica said. She had no vision, so nothing could interfere with it.

When class was over, Sylvie said, "I guess we should meet in front of school at dismissal."

Veronica agreed, then excused herself to go to the bathroom, too nervous to talk further.

Mistaken Identity

After last bell, Veronica went outside half expecting Sylvie not to be there. But Sylvie was by the front door, waiting.

"I thought we would go get the plants first," Sylvie said. She was standing in a sun patch acting perfectly normal, like doing time with Veronica Louise Weirdo Morgan was no big deal.

Veronica followed Sylvie down Madison Avenue like a dog on a long leash, while the other Randolf girls hung around outside the building catching the first warm rays of sun. In a million years, Veronica would not have predicted she would ever be following Sylvie Samuels home.

They walked over to Lexington, and two blocks from Paws and Claws, Sylvie led them into a plant store. Veronica hung back, trying to figure out how she could run down and say hello. But then she remembered there would never be a reason to go to Paws and Claws again.

"Hello, ladies, what I can do you for?" a small old man in a gray smock said. His thinning hair was slicked back. He leaned to one side and Veronica wagered if she looked, she would find that he had a hump on his back. His resemblance to the laboratory assistant of Dr. Frankenstein was uncanny.

"We would like to buy two plants, please," Sylvie said. "Two of the same of any type of plant, as long as they are similar in size and health and appearance."

"One for you and one for your sister. Is that the idea?" the man asked.

"No," Sylvie said.

"No?" said the man.

"No, we aren't sisters. Although we do need two plants. We're using them for a science experiment so it is important that the two plants resemble each other as much as possible."

"Come on," he said, "you're pulling my leg. She's pulling my leg, right? You look exactly the same. You're not identical twins?"

He stepped back and gave Veronica and Sylvie the once-over. Then, as though an amazing thought occurred to him, he declared, "You're even wearing the same clothes!"

Obviously he had never heard of school uniforms before.

"I can assure you," Sylvie said in a very adult manner,

which Veronica couldn't help but be impressed by, "we are not sisters."

Veronica paid for her African violet with a sweaty twenty-dollar bill her parents had given her that morning as recompense for the lousy mess they'd made of her life while Mary was away. She stuffed the change in the front pocket of her backpack.

Latchkey Kid

Sylvie Samuels had her own keys and her own life after school that did not involve any grown-ups.

Veronica would be so sad without Mary. Wonderful, kind, loving Mary, Mary who was alone in the Hospital for Special Surgery. Sylvie did not have a Mary. Or maybe they were alone in the Samuels apartment because they were supposed to complete their science projects without any help from parents or other outside sources. Veronica had concluded that Randolf students had gotten a lot of help on their projects in the past and this year the teachers were cracking down.

But from the way Sylvie flipped on the lights, put her book bag down, and seemed so at ease, Veronica could tell Sylvie came home to an empty apartment every day.

"Oh. Do you mind taking your shoes off?" Sylvie asked. "And just hang your coat in the closet." She hung up her coat and disappeared into some other part of the apartment.

Veronica stood in the front hall, dismayed. What did she expect? A tour of the house? She took her coat off and opened the closet. Maybe no one else would find a coat closet with space for coats unusual, but Veronica did. The Morgan coat closet was like a gag from a Marx Brothers movie. Everything from tennis rackets to boxes of holiday cards—fully addressed and stamped but never sent—to art projects Veronica had made in kindergarten was stuffed in there. You opened that door at your own risk. Mr. Morgan had opened it about a year ago and was promptly hit on the nose by a sand wedge from an old set of golf clubs. No one even knew who those golf clubs belonged to. The Morgans had hung their coats on hooks outside the closet ever since.

Veronica took off her shoes, not knowing where to go. Sylvie wasn't a very good hostess. She took her backpack, wandered into the living room, and plopped down on a long beige couch amid the craziest assortment of pillows. She loved all the patterns, stripes, and tribal designs mixed with paisleys and so many colors. Some living rooms looked like rooms people were supposed to get out of before getting comfortable in, but not this one. She nestled into the pillows and pulled a paisley cashmere throw that hung over the back of the couch around her. She wished her house could be like this, filled with nice things, but not cluttered. Marion Morgan collected everything.

Sylvie made a lot of clanging noises. She must be in the

kitchen. Veronica missed Mary desperately and wanted her Oreos. At lunch, she hadn't had much of an appetite and now she was sitting in a stranger's living room with a stomach roaring like a lion. She covered her tummy with a striped pillow.

There was a table to her right with a few photographs of Sylvie and her parents. They weren't recent. It was the same in Veronica's house. Parents seemed to lose interest in documenting their lives as their children got older. Like the novelty of having a family just wore off or something. Sylvie's mother was much younger than Veronica's mother. She was also very pretty.

Sylvie called. Veronica followed her voice into a breakfast nook off the kitchen. It had a window that faced an airshaft. From Sylvie's window, you could see into the apartments on the other two sides of the airshaft. It was like having rows of television sets that played the stories of real people's lives.

At the moment, most of the rooms Veronica could see were dark and empty. But a few had life in them. A housekeeper vacuumed in one. An old man read the newspaper in another. Veronica was wondering about the other people and their lives when Sylvie set a platter of scrambled eggs and toast down on the table.

"Are you hungry?" Sylvie asked. She handed Veronica a fork and a napkin.

"Sort of," Veronica said, praying the growling of her stomach wouldn't betray her. She wanted to eat slowly, but honestly, scrambled eggs had never tasted so good. And the toast, for some strange reason, was the most satisfying food she had ever eaten. She should remember to tell Mary that this would be a good snack from now on. When they were finished eating, Veronica followed Sylvie and watched her put their dishes in the dishwasher.

"I guess we should start our project," Sylvie said after everything was cleaned up. She opened a cabinet and took out a pile of neatly folded newspapers. She spread them out on one of the counters.

"What kind of chemicals do you want to put in?" Sylvie asked. She turned over one of the pots and dumped out a plant, separating the soil from the roots.

"I don't know, ammonia and bleach?" Veronica said, immediately regretting it. Dr. Snope would call that kind of comment "provocative."

Sylvie rummaged around the kitchen displaying no sign of provocation whatsoever. "I was thinking we could put in cleaning things that wouldn't, like, gas us out of the house," she said.

"Okay, I guess that's the more sensible approach," Veronica said. Sylvie examined rows upon rows of products: Ajax, Windex, silver polish, and Fantastik.

"Should we just use them all?" Sylvie asked.

"Sure," Veronica said by default.

Sylvie piled everything on the counter and Veronica followed her lead, pouring and spraying and sprinkling the pile of soil. It reminded Veronica of potion making, an activity mothers detested because it was so messy, but there was no one at Sylvie's house to object. After Veronica poured a pile of borax over the mixture, Sylvie squirted silver polish into the middle. The container made a noise like a fart. She did it again. Was she trying to be funny? Veronica didn't want to laugh, just in case Sylvie had done it by accident. Instead she dumped a pile of Ajax in the middle and stirred it around with a wooden spoon. She threw all caution to the wind and unscrewed the spray nozzle from the Fantastik and poured a big stream into their soil. It was more fun than she had had in weeks. She and Sylvie were up to their elbows in soil. When it was thoroughly blended Sylvie showed Veronica how to put a few rocks at the bottom of the new pots for drainage and how to repot the plants. One plant got fresh and clean potting soil. The other one got the contaminated mixture.

Sylvie put the contaminated plant in the linen closet and turned off the light. Veronica suggested they put the other plant by a window. She hoped the window Sylvie chose would be in some other part of the apartment she hadn't seen yet. But Sylvie thought it best to put it in the living room.

"This is the sunniest spot in the house," she said. They went back to the kitchen and scrubbed their hands with a nailbrush. It took half a bottle of soap to get clean.

Mrs. Morgan picked up Veronica at six o'clock.

"Bye, Veronica. This was fun," Sylvie said.

"It was," Veronica said. "See you tomorrow."

Recovery

What do you give a woman waking up from hip surgery? A whoopee cushion? A pile of rubber vomit? A Mylar balloon? The gift shop in the hospital where Mary's hip had been replaced was filled with inappropriate gifts. Veronica would have liked to get Mary a stuffed animal but the selection seemed more appropriate for four-year-old girls than sturdy Mary. Plus she couldn't look at anything that resembled a puppy. Mr. and Mrs. Morgan were patient while Veronica selected a gossip magazine, a book of crossword puzzles, and a box of chocolates. She brought them to the register, assigning each member of the family a gift, but her parents were nice and said all the presents could be from her.

The Morgans waited in the solarium until Mary woke up from her anesthesia. They took turns feeding dollar bills into the vending machines and devouring Doritos, Snickers, and stale granola bars.

"Is it taking too long?" Veronica asked. She was on her second bag of Doritos.

"Don't worry, darling. Mary will be fine," Mrs. Morgan said.

"She'd better be," Mr. Morgan said, "or we will never eat a proper meal again."

Veronica knew that was supposed to be funny, but her father's jokes had never been easy to laugh at. That in itself used to make her laugh. Now it just made her sad. Since losing Cadbury nothing was particularly funny.

When Mary woke up, Veronica was so happy she had to stop herself from crawling into her bed. The hospital had washed Mary with some kind of antiseptic and she smelled different. But Veronica kissed her a dozen times because she was alive.

"I made it," Mary said, still groggy from the anesthesia. She had tears in her eyes.

Veronica squeezed Mary's hand and said, "See, Mary, you are tougher than you think."

"So are you, my baby. So are you." Mary smiled and told Mrs. Morgan to open the drawer of her nightstand. Inside was a menu from Grand Szechuan.

"It is supposed to be excellent. And I am hungry."

"Hungry is good!" Mr. Morgan exclaimed. Veronica, who was sick to death of Chinese food, was so happy she thought she would burst. This was as good an end to a day as possible. Thank God for her family.

Silence Is Golden

Mary was recovering well and Veronica's project with Sylvie was progressing. The changes in the plants were becoming visible. It had been Sylvie's idea to rob one plant of light by putting it in a closet and rob it of nourishment by feeding it poison, but it had been Veronica's idea to rob the plant emotionally. Every day while Sylvie cooked, Veronica opened the closet and sneered at her plant. She gave it dirty looks and said mean things to it. She told it it was weird. She told it it didn't fit in. She told it she didn't like it. She wished she was talking to some of her classmates. They made her feel bad just because she cared that her dog died. Well, the worst thing that had probably ever happened to any of them was having a stupid cashmere sweater cut in half.

Every day after they ate, Sylvie loaded the dishwasher while Veronica sponged up. Then they brought the closet plant out and put it next to the window plant. Veronica drew pictures of the plants, charting any changes in their appearance. And Sylvie made notations of the changes on a graph. Veronica was comfortable at Sylvie's. When she used to go to Cricket's house she talked all the time, about anything. She remembered once being so desperate for a topic she actually went on and on about fingernails because she was certain that if Cricket got bored, Cricket wouldn't invite her over again. Veronica enjoyed that talking wasn't required when she was with Sylvie.

Sylvie's parents obviously worked a lot, because they were never home. Veronica hadn't met either of them. It was strange how the absence of authority inspired such good habits. She and Sylvie could have goofed off all afternoon. But they never did. Mary always made Veronica sit up straight at her desk to do her homework but Sylvie insisted on working at the coffee table sitting on the floor. Veronica liked being on the floor too. The drawing part of science was fun. She had just invented a way of layering similar colors to create a kind of 3-D effect. Coloring used to frustrate Veronica because the colors that were in her pencil sets were so limited and nature never was. Yes, the leaves of plants were green and the bark of trees was brown but leaves were about twenty different greens and bark was so many colors. But as a reward for her hard work on the Carver family apologies, her parents had given her a new set of colored pencils with over one hundred colors.

When the doorman buzzed up saying that Mrs. Morgan was in the lobby, Veronica was startled. She had no idea it had gotten so late.

Fifth Avenue was noisy with the sounds of rush hour surging around them. Buses, cars, and bicycles seemed to be veering in and out of every empty space. It was always such a shock to reenter the world after Sylvie's.

On the way home, Mrs. Morgan asked, "What do you do there? I'm dying to know if you're beginning to get a sense of her."

"She makes good snacks," Veronica said.

"That's interesting. Such as?" her mother asked, and smoothed Veronica's hat down over her ears in a way Veronica hated.

"Today we had grilled cheese sandwiches and a salad with pears and walnuts."

"That does sound good," Mrs. Morgan said.

Veronica shifted her backpack and put her hand inside her mother's. Sometimes holding hands made her mother stop asking so many questions. Veronica didn't feel like talking.

Halfway

The closet plant was no longer just wilting and turning yellow. It was all but dead.

"You are so pretty," Veronica said to the thriving plant. "No one likes you," she said to the dying plant.

Sylvie set the table and Veronica wondered if she always made food like this for herself or if she was trying to make a good impression. If she was, it was working.

"Are you, like, really into food or something?" Veronica asked.

"I love cooking," Sylvie said. "It's like arts and crafts you can eat."

Veronica didn't know any other eleven-year-old who made food like Sylvie did. Today Sylvie had prepared pumpkin ravioli with brown butter. Veronica wondered if her mother liked pumpkin ravioli. It seemed like something her mother would like. But she would want to get it in the fall and from the farmers' market. Her mother loved things that were seasonal and not available all the time. Sylvie said the sauce was just butter, but browned.

"Doesn't your mother cook?" Veronica asked.

"No," Sylvie said. "She's dead. She died when I was three."

"Oh. I'm sorry," Veronica said, stunned. "I don't know what to say," was all she could manage.

"Sometimes," Sylvie said, "and I don't mean this in a mean way, Veronica, but sometimes there is nothing to say. That's why I don't talk much."

Veronica believed Sylvie didn't mean it in a mean way, but she still felt like she'd been told off. Talking too much ran in her family.

She wanted to hug Sylvie, to compliment her, to say something. But she didn't know how to express anything that would be worth expressing, so she took Sylvie's advice and didn't say anything. She rinsed the silverware instead.

At home she couldn't take her eyes off her parents. Her parents who she took for granted and complained about all the time. They both drove her crazy. But that was her life: two kinds of craziness and knowing that she was loved. Poor Sylvie.

"Mary called your mother and me today," Mr. Morgan said. "She's doing wonderfully and apparently giving the nurses a run for their money."

"She asked about you, honey. She misses you," Mrs. Morgan said. "Do you think you can make it at Sylvie's for one more week?"

"I guess so," Veronica said.

"Has it been awful?" her father asked.

"No," Veronica answered. It hadn't been awful at all, but she didn't care to elaborate. She couldn't stop thinking about Sylvie. Sylvie who cooked for herself and who cooked so well for Veronica, Sylvie who didn't talk much. Sylvie who didn't have a mother.

The Light at the End of the Hall

Veronica and Sylvie decided to arrange their data like a graphic novel. Veronica's sketches would go in the panels and Sylvie would add all the data in a manner that was both scientific and narrative. Veronica couldn't help but feel the plants were telling a bigger story.

She was very conscientiously outlining each frame, and the care she put into making them reminded her of the way she used to put dashes between each letter in each word she spelled when she was in kindergarten. Her mother had tried to make her see that instead of adding clarity, she was making her writing illegible. But Veronica never saw it that way.

She had one more frame to make when the lead of her pencil broke. She dug into her pencil case and came up empty. "Oh, no," Veronica said, "I broke my lead."

"There's a sharpener in my room," Sylvie said without looking up.

Veronica left the living room wondering what strange things lurked in the uncharted areas of the Samuelses' apartment. Maybe showing people around your apartment was the behavior of grown-ups. Her mother always took people on tours of their apartment and got so excited to go on tours of other people's. Kids generally didn't do that. But still, it was strange to have spent every day here and not know anything about what was beyond the living room. She'd never actually been anywhere except the living room, a powder room, and the kitchen.

Veronica made her way down the hall. Toward the end was a light, like someone had left a TV on, which struck her as odd. But this light was many colors. It throbbed and bounced off the wall, which made the source impossible to identify. What was it: a lava lamp? An interactive artwork? She was mildly disappointed to discover the source of all these colors was just an ordinary laptop.

On the desk in Sylvie's room an open laptop played a slide show. Each image held for a second or two before morphing into the next. Sylvie's life was exposed for Veronica to examine.

Some babies look like old men when they are born. Sylvie was adorable. And the way her mother gazed upon her was startling. There was so much love in her eyes, so much joy in her face. None of the pictures of Veronica and her mother had that kind of mother-daughter-precious-moment-captured-forever-on-film quality because Mr. Morgan took the pictures and it always took him so long to operate the camera that by the time he finally pressed the button, whatever spontaneity had prompted the picture in the first place was long gone.

The pictures on Sylvie's laptop told a beautiful story, but it was too short. The oldest Sylvie looked in the pictures was two or three. The last picture of them together was taken at a beach. They were standing in the surf holding hands. And even though the picture was taken from behind, Veronica was certain they were smiling.

Veronica understood now that Sylvie Samuels wasn't weird or cold or creepy. Sylvie had a hole in her heart where her love used to be. Sylvie Samuels was sad, just like Veronica.

The Right Moment

That night Veronica hid her flashlight and all her colored pencils in bed. After her parents turned off the lights she set up shop. She copied Esme's Rainbow Bridge story for Sylvie. She made each line a different color and it took a long time.

The next day after school, they met up as usual. Veronica wondered when the right moment would present itself. She had an idea that there would be a perfect time for giving the story to Sylvie. She considered handing it to her when they were waiting for the light on the corner of Ninety-Sixth and Third. But there was so much traffic and it was so loud she thought better of it.

When they got to Sylvie's building and Sylvie was busy in the lobby opening the mailbox with her little key, Veronica fished the story out of her backpack. And while they stood next to each other in the elevator, watching the numbers light up as it climbed, Veronica worked up the courage to hand it to Sylvie.

The minute the story was out of Veronica's hand she

knew it was the dumbest thing she'd ever done in her whole life. How could she have compared a dead animal to a dead mother? How could she have used so many bright colors and glitter? What was wrong with her? No wonder she had no friends.

Veronica watched Sylvie read the story, wondering if their short friendship was over. But when Sylvie was finished reading, she hugged Veronica.

"Oh God, I thought you were going to hate it. It feels corny now—like a greeting card."

"Yeah, but I'm corny."

"Oh God," Veronica said again. She couldn't think of anything else to say.

"There has to be somewhere they go," Sylvie said. "It can't be the end of my mom. I don't believe in heaven exactly, but there has to be somewhere they go. I think they are waiting for us."

"I hope so," Veronica said. She hadn't thought she would see Cadbury again, but that was the point of the Rainbow Bridge, after all. "Maybe they're together."

"Maybe my mom is playing with your dog," Sylvie said. The elevator reached the ninth floor and the doors opened.

It was nicer to imagine that Cadbury was waiting for her instead of focusing on how miserable she was without him. Maybe behind Sylvie's deadpan personality was a glass that was half-full.

After eating and cleaning up, the girls examined the leaves of the healthy plant.

"Why does Auden Georges always get such good grades?" Veronica asked. "I read her Monet paper. No offense, but I thought it was boring."

"It was. All her work is. But what it lacks in creativity it makes up for with accuracy. Teachers like that. Go figure."

Sylvie had gone to school with Auden Georges since kindergarten, so she should know.

"Time to make our freshly contaminated water," Sylvie said. Veronica and Sylvie had developed an actual recipe, which they measured and made fresh each day. As research scientists, they had to be consistent.

"I bet her parents beat her if she doesn't do better than everyone else. Why else would she cry when she doesn't get a perfect grade? She is worse than Melody that way," Sylvie said.

Veronica doubted Sylvie had any idea how important doing well on this project was for her credibility. Auden Georges didn't have to worry about credibility. Her English accent always made her credible. But Veronica was in a full-blown credibility crisis.

"I feel like a murderer," Veronica said, pouring the poison water on the closet plant. It was Friday and Veronica hoped the closet plant would die over the weekend so when they handed the project in on Monday their results would be crystal clear. It made her feel mean. She had hurt the plant's feelings daily and robbed it of all nutrition. She was a plant murderer. That was how badly she wanted a good grade.

"Wow, your sketches are so good, Veronica," Sylvie said.

Veronica had to agree, even though what Sylvie was admiring were just the minisketches. She'd made bigger, better ones for the graphic novel presentation.

"Can I see them for a minute?" Veronica handed the sketchbook to Sylvie, and Sylvie flipped through it, making the pictures of the plants come to life. "Are you thinking what I'm thinking?" Sylvie said.

"I don't know, what are you thinking?"

"A flipbook!" Sylvie flipped each page with her thumb and their entire experiment sprang to life before their eyes. Veronica had been very careful to measure exactly equal quadrants on her paper and had put her illustrations inside each quadrant. By cutting the pages into four squares and attaching them, they could make their graphic novel into a perfect flipbook. Veronica was psyched.

Sylvie kept flipping the pages.

"That is exactly my life this year," Veronica said as the closet plant died again and again before her eyes.

"It is?" Sylvie said.

"Yup. I was all alive and vital and then people ignored me and were mean and I wilted."

"You have a funny way of looking at things," Sylvie said.

Veronica was incensed.

"I remember you from the first day," Sylvie said. "Your parents were so friendly and you just stood there looking at me like you hated me. Sort of like you're doing right now."

Veronica did nearly hate Sylvie right now. "But you didn't say anything to me," she said.

"You didn't say anything to me either. And you had everything a person could want—two parents, for starters, who were taking you to school. My dad hasn't had time to take me to school in years."

Veronica remembered that morning too. But the way she remembered it, Sylvie wasn't the new girl. Veronica thought it was up to Sylvie to be nice and say hello first. When Sylvie didn't, she assumed Sylvie didn't like her. But Mary always said things weren't as they appeared, and obviously there was a whole other side to the story that Veronica hadn't even considered. The side that was not her side. Oops. She didn't ponder that side as often as she should.

Sylvie got up and returned with a dilapidated Barbie doll. She put it on the coffee table for Veronica to examine. Its face was filthy, it was missing a leg, and its hair, what was left of it, was matted and tangled. The doll had lots of empty holes along its scalp where tufts of its hair were missing. It was a mess.

"I just had an idea," Sylvie said. "Do you have any Barbies?"

"I don't know if I still do," Veronica said. "Why?" Part of her didn't even want to talk to Sylvie. She was so embarrassed by her assessment of their first meeting.

"Our experiment shows what happens to a plant when it is not treated right, right? Well, we could hypothesize that people are the same way. If you treat a plant badly and ignore its needs it dies, so the same would happen to a person. If you mistreat a person it ends up like this Barbie."

Just like me, thought Veronica. "Oh, Sylvie, I love it. If I can't find a Barbie, I will buy one and it can be the happy, popular Barbie who is treated well and yours can be the sad misfit Barbie. Can we somehow implicate Sarah-Lisa Carver in this theory?" Veronica asked.

"That is hilarious, Veronica. You threw a shoe at that girl and cut her sweaters to bits and you want her to be the mean one?"

"Okay, fine! I won't implicate Sarah-Lisa. I'll take a more humanitarian approach. But I still want to make little Randolf uniforms. What if I made little uniforms?"

"You don't mind working over the weekend?"

"I want to work over the weekend!" Veronica said.

"Me too," Sylvie said.

They sealed the deal with another hug. It was awesome.

I'm Afraid to Tell You

Veronica rifled through her room looking for a Barbie doll. She dug in drawers, old crates, and under her bed. She could see the doll in her mind, but she couldn't remember where it was. It was so frustrating.

"Mom!" she yelled at the top of her lungs. She had to yell, she was under her bed.

"I'm right here, Veronica! Don't shout!" her mother shouted. "Honey! I can't hear a word you're saying. Come in the kitchen!"

Oh sure. It was okay for Mrs. Morgan to yell halfway around the globe, but the rules were different for Veronica Morgan. Veronica crawled out from under her bed and walked begrudgingly into the kitchen. Her mother was standing in the middle of the room looking confused.

"I don't know what to do for dinner." She sighed. "Any ideas?" It was a silly question since they both knew the answer.

"Hunan Delight?" Veronica said.

"A girl after my own heart." Her mother moved toward the phone.

"I love you, Mommy." All of a sudden Veronica was overwhelmed by the idea of her mother dying and not being there to order Chinese food. She really was so ungrateful sometimes.

"I love you too," her mother said. "What brought this on? Is everything okay?"

"Yes. Mommy?"

"Yes, my darling."

"I want to do something with a Barbie. Didn't I used to have one? Do you know where it is?"

"You know what?" her mother said as she smoothed Veronica's hair. "I actually do. Or at least I'm pretty sure I do."

This was amazing news because organization was not her mother's strong suit. Veronica's grandmother had everything labeled and packed in plastic protective sleeves and orderly rows but she hadn't passed that gene down. Veronica's mother was very good at putting things in places and forgetting the places she had put them.

"Where?" Veronica asked.

"I'm afraid to tell you," Mrs. Morgan said.

"No," Veronica said with mock horror. *I'm afraid to tell you* was a Morgan family euphemism for the front closet.

"Yes," her mother said. "Two words. Three, actually. The. Front. Closet. There is a box in there filled with birthday gifts you never wanted. I planned on giving them to a charity. But, as usual, I haven't gotten around to it."

Veronica gave her mother a hug and ran out of the kitchen, happy she had a scatterbrained mother who was too disorganized to do things like give a box to charity.

"Please be careful in there, honey!" her mother said. "I want to eat dinner and go to bed. I'm too tired tonight to take you to the emergency room."

Veronica was sure this new part of their project, the human element, as Sylvie called it, combined with their scientific data about the plants and their drawings, would get them As. She opened the closet door slowly and pulled the string attached to the light bulb, expecting to flood the place with yellow light. But there was so much junk everywhere the light barely made a difference.

There was tall junk, short junk, junk on shelves, junk on the floor. She was surrounded by junk. Wrapping paper rolls, a set of skis (no one in her family had ever skied, as far as she knew), the lethal golf clubs. A fur coat startled her. There was an exercise machine folded up and Veronica had a vague memory of her father promising one year to get into shape (one of his particularly famous lies). There was a bunch of folding chairs they used for Passover, an ironing board, piles of board games, and on a shelf above her head bottles and bottles of wine and champagne. She pushed her way through the coats, eating a mouthful of fur in the process.

With the aid of a flashlight she found the box she was looking for. Inside was a set of dominoes, three Candy Land games—all unopened—a set of Boxcar Children books, and at the very bottom two Barbie dolls, still in their packages! She took hold of them and made her way back to civilization.

"Did you find them?" her mother shouted.

"Yes!"

"Well, good! I guess it was meant to be."

Nature vs. Nurture

Veronica was so preoccupied with how she was going to make little Randolf uniforms for the Barbie dolls, she didn't even notice at first they were eating vegetable lasagna. This was a Morgan family favorite, and a meal Veronica's mother usually kept portions of in the freezer for emergencies.

"I thought we were having Hunan Delight," Veronica said.

"I know, but as I was ordering I remembered we had it last night."

"And the night before . . ."

"I guess that's why I thought enough," Mrs. Morgan said. "For a day or two anyway. Please pass me the salad."

Veronica was still thinking about her science project. What would be the best way to display the Barbies? She hoisted herself and the enormous salad bowl down the table to her mother. No one except for Mr. Morgan could pass it to anyone without standing. The leaves of arugula in the salad gave her an idea.

"I am intrigued," her father said. "Have you and this Sylvie person become friends?"

"Yes." Veronica hadn't seen friendship with Sylvie coming, but here she was acknowledging that yes, it had arrived.

Her parents looked at each other.

"What?" Veronica asked.

"Nothing," her mother said.

"You obviously have some opinion," Veronica said. "Some theory about child development and psychoneurotic something . . ."

"No. We're just happy," her mother said.

Both parents nodded.

"How is the work going?" her father asked. He clearly thought it was adorable that his eleven-year-old daughter had work.

"Pretty good," Veronica said, chewing on a crunchy lasagna noodle, one from the top that was especially brown and crisp. The top and the sides of the lasagna were her favorite parts.

"We made a flipbook that is really cool," she told her parents.

"What is so cool about it?" her mother asked.

"Well, we had to record our observations so Sylvie took our drawings, well, mostly my drawings, and she cut them out on separate little pieces of paper and stapled the top together and made it into a flipbook. You can watch the plant die or come back to life depending on which direction you go."

"That sounds very creative," her father said.

"Lovey, do you want some more?"

"No thank you, I'm full."

"You are? Usually you eat so much of this."

"I had coq au vin at Sylvie's."

"I beg your pardon?" her father said.

"She has really weird snacks at her house," Veronica said.

"Does she have a caterer?" her father asked. "I will have more of your wonderful lasagna, Marion, thank you."

"No, Daddy. There isn't a caterer. There is no one, actually."

"Did you order out?" her mother asked.

"No! Sylvie's just a really good cook. Her mother died when she was little and it's how she entertains herself."

There was a charge in the air that meant Veronica's parents had simultaneously arrived at a number of theories about Sylvie Samuels based on the fact that her mother had died and all the case studies they'd read. It wasn't fair. They didn't even know Sylvie. But they were alive and she tried to be grateful for that.

Final Touches

On Saturday morning, Veronica was dying to call Sylvie, but she knew it was too early. She distracted herself by working on the doll uniforms. She took her blouse from Cadbury's shiva and a jumper from her closet and examined them inside and out. The jumper only had three pieces: a front and two back pieces with a zipper in the middle. She could make the doll jumpers without the zipper and use just two pieces. There were no sleeves, so that was easy. The blouse was a lot more complicated. The collar, the sleeves, the buttonholes—she wished Mary was here. Mary was a much better sewer. She put the Barbie down on a piece of loose-leaf paper and outlined it to make a pattern. Next she would cut her actual uniform and use the fabric. There was probably some Randolf rule about defacing your school uniform and a punishment to fit the crime. But too bad.

At nine o'clock, she couldn't stand it anymore and called Sylvie.

"I had an idea about how to show the Barbies," Veronica said. "Let's plant them. Do you think you can get some more pots? And more dirt?"

"That is so genius," Sylvie said. "Did you find a Barbie?"

"I did! I'm already sewing."

Veronica holed up in her room all day to make the tiny outfits. Mary would have done a much better job—but having real Randolf uniform fabric to work with helped a lot. Halfway through the first blouse she gave up on the needle and thread and used glue. It was much easier that way. She also didn't have tiny buttons so she used actual Randolf ones, but only one for each blouse.

On Sunday morning, Sylvie called. "I got the extra pots," she said. "How is the sewing going?"

"Good-ish," Veronica said. "I think we should use the same data we did for the plants, but substitute unfriendliness for chemicals, and basically copy the plant's deterioration for the Barbies."

"Is your hypothesis that the lack of nourishment, clean water, and sunlight killed the doll, or unkindness? Because I agree, we should make the Barbie part of our report as official-looking as possible so Mr. Bower will take it seriously. But I wonder if you think the dolls reflect the effect of emotions or of being fed toxic chemicals."

"Hmm, good question," Veronica said. "I guess both. Physical and mental."

"I agree."

"This is becoming very psychological. My parents will be so proud. We could leave an arm that fell off lying in the pot, like the leaves that fell off the plant," Veronica said.

"Yes!" Sylvie said. "Maybe I can try to make the whole Barbie kind of yellow and brown at the edges."

Veronica was so excited she didn't know how she would get through the rest of the day.

The Big Blastoff

Sylvie spent the night Sunday and they stayed up till midnight working. Veronica had never worked so hard on anything in her life. They called their project Nature vs. Nurture: A Tale of Two Dolls, Two Plants, and the Lives They Lived. Veronica laughed so hard when she came up with the title because Nature vs. Nurture was an expression her parents used a lot. Since she could remember, they told her all her problems were the result of genetics, not of Mr. and Mrs. Morgan's parenting. Ha. Those were the kind of jokes you got from parents who were both psychiatrists.

Mrs. Morgan sent both girls out the door on Monday morning with freshly toasted bagels. She had Charlie put them in a taxi because it was raining and they were bleary-eyed from staying up so late and they had so much to carry. There were so many bags and boxes being carried into Randolf that morning it felt like the sixth graders were celebrating Christmas, not presenting science projects. Darcy

Brown and Liv O'Malley were wrestling the giant ant farm they'd built up the stairs.

Maggie Fogel pressed herself against the wall in a state of total terror.

"They're just ants, Maggie," Becky said.

"I know! But there are so many of them!" Maggie screamed.

"They aren't alligators, you know? Even if they get out they're not going to bite you," Liv said. She and Darcy staggered down the hall with their unwieldy ant farm.

Athena and Sarah-Lisa were very helpful during all this and pretended to bite Maggie. Veronica wondered where their project was. They weren't carrying anything.

"Welcome," Mr. Bower said at the beginning of their double science period. *He must live for this day*, Veronica thought. He oohed and ahhed each team as they walked their projects in. Mr. Bower loved science the way her parents loved psychiatry. The way extremely religious people love God.

"Welcome," Mr. Bower said again and again. He kept smoothing his hair down, what little of it there was. Each team went to its assigned place and began unpacking. "You have about fifteen minutes to set up," Mr. Bower said. "Melody will hand out grading forms, because as you know, in addition to a grade from me, you will also be grading one another."

Hearing her name spoken out loud by her beloved Mr. Bower, in front of all the other girls, was almost too much for Melody. She fluttered from table to table handing out grading forms. Veronica worried she might just start rubbing up against Mr. Bower like the lonely orange cat in the boiler room.

"Please do not grade on anything other than the integrity of the idea and the workmanship behind its execution," Mr. Bower said. "Please grade your peers on interest, accuracy, and accessibility. Who can define accessibility?"

"Like, is the project showing off," Coco Weitzner said. She and Maggie were busy pouring distilled water into the chamber of a humidifier. Their project was cloud formation.

"Yes!" Mr. Bower exclaimed. "Does the project let you in or is it so interested in getting an A that it's more about fancy terminology or gadgetry or how much parents helped than it is about the subject? I want science for the people by the people."

Melody handed Veronica one of the peer grading forms. Last night, when she put the finishing touches on the uniforms, she was pretty sure her peers would think she was a genius. She thought she was a genius. But looking at the real Randolf uniforms next to her cockeyed, handmade ones, she wasn't so sure. Not to mention how dinky their pathetic plants looked next to the other projects: rubber-band-powered airplanes, cloud machines, and Lego robotic sustainable structures. Ugh. By comparison, Veronica and Sylvie's hard work seemed awfully low tech. But before she had time to think about it too much a crowd gathered around her and Sylvie, wanting to know what the Barbies were about. Thank God Randolf was an all-girls school. The Barbies were a hit.

"Are they part of your exhibit?" Selma Wong, who had never acknowledged Veronica before, asked. Veronica was honored because Selma and Auden had built the flying machine Mr. Bower was so excited about. At the end of the class they would launch it.

Sylvie also had a crowd around the flipbook. Veronica tried to see what her classmates were seeing: the flipbook, the dolls, the actual plants, and she had to admit there were so many aspects of their data and they had documented all of it. Their hard work had paid off.

Without warning, a uniformed man burst into the lab carrying a wrapped parcel. He brought it over to Athena and Sarah-Lisa's table. Everyone left the flipbook and gathered around the mysterious man. He and Sarah-Lisa exchanged words and then, very dramatically, like he was unveiling the actual *Mona Lisa*, he exposed what was underneath the paper. Sarah-Lisa jumped up and down.

"It looks so good!" she said.

The whole class clamored around Sarah-Lisa and Athena's project, which was an enormous dollhouse, complete with windows that opened and doors on hinges, an outdoor shower with running water, solar panels on the roof, and a swimming pool that apparently heated itself from the sun. Each room was filled with tiny furniture. It was the most expensive dollhouse in the world and Athena and Sarah-Lisa had had the audacity to glue small rectangles of cardboard to the outside, thinking this would make it look like they had built the whole thing by themselves.

Mr. Bower clapped his hands three times. "For the love of science! Please! Settle down! Go back to your tables."

Selma Wong cried, "I will not get an *A* anymore. Look how unprofessional my project looks now, compared to Athena and Sarah-Lisa's!"

One by one everyone's hopes collapsed. Becky and Tillie Allen's solar-powered Lego schoolhouse looked ridiculous next to the country estate of Sarah-Lisa and Athena.

Sylvie caught Veronica's eye. Who could compete with the architectural details of Sarah-Lisa and Athena's project? There were even pots on the miniature Viking stove in the kitchen.

Mr. Bower clapped his hands again, still trying to get everyone's attention. "All right, now that all projects are on display, begin your rotations. Remember the rules and grade fairly. This isn't a popularity contest."

Sylvie went first, leaving Veronica to man their station. Veronica wished they could meet in the bathroom to talk about the dollhouse! What was Mr. Bower going to do?

She tried her best to answer questions from the girls who gathered around her project but it was really hard to get that dollhouse out of her mind. No matter what the rules were, there was always a kid whose parents caved and bought them a finished project. Sometimes it was the parents, not the kids, who forced this kind of perfection. Veronica wondered if she would ever find out which way it was with Athena and Sarah-Lisa. Something about the chauffeur and how Sarah-Lisa jumped up and down made Veronica think it was her idea, not her parents'.

Becky Shickler roared with laughter when she saw the yellow wilting Barbie doll with its missing arm and its Randolf uniform. Veronica noticed her write a big *A* on her grading form.

Melody came over and said, "I really like your project. It looks like you worked really hard."

Veronica hugged her. Veronica really hoped this meant they'd made up. Melody was such a good egg.

"I'm really looking forward to checking out your biosphere," Veronica said.

Tillie Allen asked about the flipbook and Veronica demonstrated the way it showed deterioration and death if you flipped it to the right, and recovery and the return to life if you flipped it to the left.

"That's awesome!" Tillie said.

Sylvie returned for her shift and Veronica went to look at the other projects.

One of her favorites (besides her own) was Liv and Darcy's ant farm. They had painted a whole country scene with a farm. It made the ants look like they were doing things for the farm, like carrying bales of hay to the barn and sticks of butter to the kitchen. Veronica loved it. She gave them an A.

"All right, may I have your attention?" Mr. Bower said. "Ladies! Please! Selma and Auden are twisting their rubber band and lubing the loops so their plane can ascend at its scheduled takeoff."

"Are you sure we shouldn't do this on the playground, Mr. Bower?" Selma asked.

"It's raining," Mr. Bower reminded them. "I don't want your plane to be ruined. Use less tension in the windup and aim it toward the closet door. I set up blankets in there to catch it. People, gather round."

Auden was painting a glue-like substance onto some very long-looped rubber bands. When she was finished, Selma twisted them up with a little hook. The plane was quite large and Auden said it was a copy of a Korda Wakefield plane from the 1940s. It was yellow and red and Veronica liked the way they'd painted it. Mr. Bower told everyone his grandfather had flown in the original. He must have really liked his grandfather because he was unbelievably excited about the takeoff. The countdown began.

"Ten, nine, eight, seven, six, five . . ."

Veronica could feel how nervous Selma and Auden were. Auden's parents were really strict about her grades. Veronica wondered if they wanted an *A* so badly they actually built the plane for her. But the way the girls handled the rubber bands indicated that they knew what they were doing.

". . . four, three, two, one and takeoff!"

Auden let go of the plane and it rose into the air, the propeller spinning just like a real plane. Everyone applauded and Auden and Selma beamed. Mr. Bower was beside himself as the plane sailed through the air.

Sarah-Lisa was so busy whispering into Athena's ear about how great their project was that she didn't notice the plane. Athena ducked but it was too late for Sarah-Lisa, who threw up her hands and batted it away. The plane tumbled through the air and into Athena and Sarah-Lisa's country house, where it knocked the roof off and left a trail of tiny shingles and furniture and broken windows in its wake before bouncing off Mr. Bower's desk and landing softly in the salad he was snacking on. The propeller eventually stopped spinning but not before making a storm of shredded carrots and cabbage and sunflower seeds.

"Oh my God! Our project!" Sarah-Lisa said, looking at the destruction of her gorgeous country house. "Who is going to fix this?" she demanded.

Mr. Bower ran to his desk and picked up the plane like a

nervous parent whose child had just fallen off a jungle gym. He held the plane gently and carefully unwound Sarah-Lisa's hair from the propeller. He picked off the lettuce and shook the plane free of sunflower seeds. He turned it slowly in all directions looking for damage. "The wing is cracked, but we can repair it during lunch," he said, returning the plane to its builders. "Wonderful work, Selma, great job, Auden."

Then he faced Sarah-Lisa and Athena.

"You girls will have to stay in from recess today," he said, "and repair your house." Sarah-Lisa looked at Mr. Bower in disbelief.

"That's not fair, you're repairing Auden's plane," she said.

"I know Auden and Selma would be able to fix their own plane, but because I take special interest in Korda Wakefield reproductions, I'm lending a hand. Since you designed and built your house, you'll know how to repair it, right? Correct me if I'm wrong," Mr. Bower said. "Is there a problem?" He and Sarah-Lisa had a staring match and Sarah-Lisa lost.

Mr. Bower had a very strong backbone after all and Veronica Morgan might have just fallen in love with him.

Weather Patterns

"I don't believe it," Sylvie said. "They barely tried to disguise the fact that they didn't build that thing."

"They are amazing," Auden Georges said, slamming her tray down.

"Are you sure we're not just jealous?" Veronica said, because she was jealous of everything about them and her emotions in this department often hampered her ability to think clearly.

"Are you talking about that million-dollar store-bought thing that was supposed to be a handmade science project?" Darcy asked.

"Well, if you are," Coco said, "move over and make room for me." Veronica hadn't sat with so many girls in her class since her first week, back when she was under Athena's wing.

"Jealous? Veronica, did you look at that thing?" Sylvie asked.

"Yes."

"Did you look at them looking at that thing?" Sylvie said. And then she leaned in and said very quietly, "They don't even know what that thing is. I asked Athena if the water was solar heated on the third floor and she had no idea."

"Mr. Bower seemed so impressed. It's so unfair," Selma said, staring at her noodles. "It's half our grade. For the whole year."

It was like being a kid in a candy store. Hearing her own fears and suspicions coming out of other people's mouths was delicious. Veronica grinned at Sylvie across the table.

"You guys," Sylvie said, "none of it matters. Mr. Bower is totally onto them. I bet they're going to have to hand in another project. One that they actually made themselves, not one that their parents paid for."

Melody arrived and put her tray next to Veronica's.

"Are you talking about Athena and Sarah-Lisa? They make me so mad," Melody declared. There was no question mark. It was a statement!

"I propose a toast," Veronica said. She raised her milk container in the air. "First, to Melody Jenkins, the hardest-working friend I have ever had. I'm sorry I did not help you at all with our Monet project and I'm glad you had a worthy partner for science. Your project was awesome."

Melody blushed. Veronica hoped she hadn't embarrassed her too much, but she really did think the biosphere Melody and her partner had made was amazing.

"Hear, hear," Sylvie said, "let's toast all the people here and everywhere in Randolf who worked hard on their science projects. Let us be acknowledged."

Milk cartons crisscrossed the table as everyone toasted.

"Cheers!" Darcy said.

"Hear, hear!" everyone said. Veronica felt like she and Sylvie were the leaders of a new generation of Randolf girls: girls who weren't afraid of the A Team, regardless of how popular they were.

In the Closet World

Mary had been home for two weeks now and really did seem better than new. Veronica and Sylvie had been coming to Veronica's for a change.

"All right, what you like for snack?" Mary asked the girls.

"Can we have Oreos?" Sylvie asked. "And bananas?"

"Of course, my baby," Mary said.

Veronica was always surprised that Sylvie enjoyed plain old Oreos and bananas over all the complicated things she made for herself at home.

"It is such a beautiful day. You should go to the park," Mary said as she peeled the bananas. "Run around. Exercise your hips! Why do you stay inside all the time?"

"We have stuff we have to do here," Veronica said.

They took the tray and went to her room. Sylvie always went straight to where Cadbury's ashes were.

"Can I tell you a secret?" Sylvie asked. She put her backpack on the floor and made herself comfortable at the foot of Veronica's nightstand.

"Sure," Veronica said. She sat next to her and put the Oreos between them.

"I have my mom's ashes too. Or some of them."

Veronica hadn't seen them. She had only seen the clothes. Sylvie had an entire closet filled with her mother's clothes, which she planned on wearing as soon as they fit her. But Veronica had never seen her ashes.

"But that's not the secret," Sylvie said. "When we scattered her ashes, after she died, I kind of ate some of them." It felt like Sylvie wanted Veronica to say something. "You did?" was all she could come up with.

"The ashes got all over my hands and under my fingernails. When we got back my dad told me to wash my hands before dinner but I didn't want her to go down the drain. So I rubbed what was left on my hands as hard as I could hoping it would go into my skin. And later that night I was biting my nails and I thought, Oh my God, I am eating my mother."

"So, she's, like, inside you," Veronica said. She knew she should be grossed out. But Sylvie opened Veronica's mind in ways that surprised her.

"Yeah. I guess."

Cadbury's ashes had been on the table next to her bed for a couple of months now. It made sense that Sylvie had scattered her mother's ashes. There were probably more rules about what to do after you lost someone that important.

They spent their afternoons playing a game they had invented: Truth or Wish.

Today Sylvie went first. She chose truth.

"Okay," Veronica asked, "are you mad every day that your mother died?"

"Yes-ish," Sylvie said. "But maybe bad things happen to people so that when they meet other people who something bad happened to they can be friends."

Veronica thought that was the nicest thing anyone had ever said. Probably the nicest thing anyone had ever said to anyone in the whole world. Once again, she had no words to express her appreciation for this friendship. She might as well have been mute. She wondered if she did anything that made Sylvie feel this special. She really hoped so.

Since Sylvie had started coming over, blankets and pillows and various knickknacks had found their way into Veronica's room, becoming part of a secret world created inside her closet.

"We're like the Boxcar Children," Sylvie said, sitting down at the makeshift table they had built on the closet floor.

"Except you are a much better cook than any of those girls," Veronica said.

"That's because they never cooked. They just ate bread and milk and berries. By the third book I was so sick of their meals. Hand me that pillow, will you?" Sylvie shifted pillows around the floor until she was comfortable.

"If you could have one wish, Sylvie, what would it be?"

"To talk to dead people," Sylvie said. "Then it wouldn't really matter so much that they were dead."

"Okay," Veronica said. "In here we can." She took Sylvie's hands and told her to close her eyes. Veronica did not like to think about Cadbury because it made her sad, but for some reason she loved thinking about Sylvie's mom. She had spent so much time at Sylvie's looking at her photographs and touching her things, it was like she had gotten to know her a little bit. She closed her eyes and re-created Sylvie's mother's face in her mind.

"Okay, I am talking to your mother," Veronica said. "She loves you so much and she also wants you to get a real haircut, at a real place. She said the place on Lexington and Sixty-Fourth is good."

"What else is she saying?"

"She adores you and is proud of you every single second of every single day and she enjoyed your science project. She also said she has been spending a lot of time with Princess Diana, who also thinks you need a proper haircut."

Sylvie giggled.

"More," she demanded. "Who else is she hanging out with?"

"John Lennon. He likes your hair this way, but he thinks

you should wear glasses. He wrote a song about you yesterday and he would also really like to meet me."

"Oh my God!" Sylvie yelled.

"What? Are you okay?"

"Cadbury just told me to tell you he is eating the most delicious bone right now and he still loves you."

A Net Is There

On a Friday morning in mid-April, Veronica's mother burst into her daughter's room.

"Lovey, wake up. Hurry. I overslept."

Veronica could barely open one eye, let alone two. She was supposed to be out the door in five minutes and her body felt like lead. It would not cooperate. She could hardly swing her feet over the side of her bed, and when she finally did, they did not want to support her weight. Veronica dressed like a robot that was running out of power. The second she was dressed, her mother pushed her out the front door with a bagel and a paper towel.

If you were late for Morning Meeting, you weren't let into the auditorium. It was almost the only consequence the school had that resembled shaming. Veronica wanted to hurry, but Fifth Avenue was surprisingly empty of people and peaceful. Thickly scented hyacinth buds were pushing their way open. There was nothing like that smell. Veronica stopped and stuck her nose right into one of the tight purple bundles.

If she stood there all day she bet she would actually see one open all the way like in a stop-motion animation. The daffodils and the tulips would be next to bloom. Several times over the winter bulbs had started to open. (What was a flower to do when the temperature was in the seventies, even in January?) And every time she saw them stick their little heads up, months too early, she wished she could tell them to go back underground. She wished she could warn them that it wasn't really spring yet, only an illusion of spring due to global warming. Today, though, it was safe. Spring was really here and the flowers would survive.

The doors to the auditorium were already closed when Veronica arrived at school. A small group of other latecomers, led by Mrs. Zarosh, the bookbinding teacher for the high school, were making their own meeting. Veronica sat down next to Mrs. Zarosh and like everyone else she put her hands into the hands of the people on either side of her. Mrs. Zarosh's hand was warm.

Silent reflection in such a small group was very intimate. Since there was no leader, Veronica thought about last week's meeting, in which Mrs. Harrison had said, "Each of us is part of the whole." She remembered Mrs. Harrison telling them to concentrate on their breathing. In. And then out. In and then out. Over and over breathing deeper and deeper until she disappeared into a kind of trance. Someone tapped her on the shoulder and she startled. Standing over her was Athena Mindendorfer.

Images from Sarah-Lisa's party shuffled through her mind like a deck of cards. She moved over to make room for Athena as the people in the circle had done for her minutes earlier. Athena sat down and took Veronica's hand.

Veronica couldn't stop thinking about the fact that she was sitting on the floor holding hands with Athena Mindendorfer. Athena smiled and Veronica smiled back. Her breathing joined Athena's breath and Mrs. Zarosh's breath and everyone else's in the circle. Together they formed a mysterious lullaby. The sun, the stones, the animals, the spirit, and the sparkling stars of Morning Verse came to her mind. No one was really ever completely alone. If you could reach out, there was always a hand to hold, somewhere in the world.

When she got home from school her mother was actually making dinner. She'd had a light day, she said. She was cracking eggs into a bowl to make carbonara. Veronica passed her mother the pepper grinder. "Thank you, lovey," she said. Her mother twisted it, making pepper fall on their dinner like black snow. "Mrs. Ferguson came over. They're back from Florida earlier than planned. She says Fitzy is eager to see you. Will you put the salad on the table?"

Veronica lugged the enormous salad bowl to the table. She hadn't thought of Fitzy for months. Did Fitzy know what had happened to Cadbury?

"Also, I invited Sylvie and her father for Passover dinner. They said they'd love to come."

Fitzy was back. Veronica didn't know if she was ready for that.

Passover

"*Baruch ata Adonai*," Mr. Morgan said. He struck a long wooden match and lit the candles with much fanfare. "*Elohaynu melech Ha-olam, asher kideshanu be-mitzvotav, ve-tzinanu-le-hadlik ner shel Yom Tov.* Welcome, Sylvie, welcome, Stuart. We're so happy to have you!"

Her father was clearly determined to give Sylvie and her dad, who had never been to a Seder, the best Seder ever. He was being so dramatic Veronica felt like they were in a production of *Fiddler on the Roof.* Ugh. "Passover," he explained, "tells the story of the Jewish people's journey into freedom. But tonight we use Egypt as a metaphor for conflict because we live in perpetual yin yang. Freedom, for example, is an undisputed right, yet human rights are exploited all the time. We crave stability. We seek reliability. And yet many also feel a pull, a need to wander, to explore. And the conflict of all conflicts: pain. Without pain we cannot understand joy." He looked over at his daughter as he raised his glass. She thought of Cadbury, who had left behind a memory so tender and so raw. "Oy," he said. "Let us raise our glasses to the perpetual paradox called the human condition." Veronica and Sylvie drank red grape juice, while the adults drank dark red wine.

Mr. Morgan held up a ramekin of salt water and Passover 101 continued. "And what we do is, we take a little piece of vegetable off the seder plate and dip it in the salt water. The salt water is a symbol of sweat and tears. Because we want to remind ourselves that although Jews were freed by the Pharaoh, Egyptians suffered for that freedom and all around the world today, people are still enslaved." Mr. Morgan dipped a piece of celery in the salt water and indicated for everyone else to do the same. Veronica chewed and swallowed years of affliction. She loved how Passover was both symbolic and actual, legend and current events.

"In the center of the table we have a nice stack of matzoh," Marvin said with obvious pleasure. "Veronica, my firstborn, why do we eat matzoh on Passover?"

Veronica decided not to point out that she was her father's only born child. "When the Jews were escaping to freedom," she said, "they didn't think they had time to wait for bread to rise. So this is what they came up with. Matzoh." She pointed at the matzoh like a contestant on a game show. Behind this curtain: a new car!

"Precisely," Mr. Morgan said with tremendous pride. His brow was wet and his jacket was a little tight, but he looked so moved by the sight of his wife, his daughter, by Mary and by their guests, Veronica thought he might cry. He flipped through his Haggadah and talked himself down. "Okay, matzoh, poverty, affliction, slavery. Check. I'm lost, Marion. Where are we?"

"Page fifteen," his wife said. Veronica looked at her mother, convinced they saw the same emotion in her father.

"Okay," he said. "Page fifteen. Traditionally, the youngest at the table asks the Four Questions. But, Sylvie, we'd be honored if you would."

Veronica had been the youngest at the table for so long she realized tonight she took that honor for granted. It was with bittersweet pleasure she sat back and listened. She felt like all the girls in her class who say Morning Verse every day but may not actually hear what they're saying.

"Why is this night different from all other nights?" Sylvie asked. "Why on this night do we only eat matzoh, but on other nights we eat bread or matzoh? Why on this night do we only eat bitter herbs and vegetables? Why on this night do we dip our herbs not once, but twice? Why on this night do we eat in a reclining position?"

"One of my favorite parts about Judaism," Mr. Morgan said, "is the importance of questions. There is no other religion I am aware of that invites argument and discussion the way we do. We love it." He looked at his wife and daughter as though all they did was argue. "I love it because being able to ask questions means you're free. And as long as you have someone to ask, it means you aren't alone." Mr. Morgan adjusted his yarmulke.

He certainly had a lot of knowledge and love for something he pretended not to care about. Why did he try so hard not to care? So many things about his heritage seemed to make him happy.

"Next on this page: the Four Children, page sixteen."

Veronica turned the page in her Haggadah. Sometimes the Seder felt like it lasted for twelve hours and no one could stop their stomach from growling and their mind from wandering. Sylvie and her father seemed totally engaged, and Veronica was relieved.

"Now, if I may confess: this was the part of the Seder I struggled with year after year," Mr. Morgan said. He was really on a roll tonight, riffing and improvising, and Veronica tried not to smile because if she did, she might laugh. "My younger brother always asked the Four Questions, and so year after year, I had to talk about the Four Children. The wise child was characterized as good because he believed in God and Passover, the wicked child was an atheist and unworthy of the freedom granted to the rest of the Jews. The simple one was boring. And the last one was so dumb, he didn't even ask a question. I knew my father didn't think I was the wise one. I was supposed to be one of the other three, and I didn't like any of them. Was I the fool? The wicked one? The simple one? I always felt set up."

Veronica knew her father's side of the family was pretty religious, but her father's parents had died before she was born and he didn't discuss them much. Her uncle actually lived in Israel and rarely came to the United States.

"So, as an adult Reform Jewish psychiatrist and a father in my own house," her father continued, "I offer this: we are all the Four Children represented at Passover. Sometimes we're clever, sometimes we're evil, sometimes we're curious, sometimes we are so content we don't need to ask anything."

Marion smiled warmly at her husband. They had met at a Seder in college. Veronica really hoped they weren't going to talk about that.

"The yin and the constant yang is itself a very Jewish idea. It's why you break a glass at a wedding: to remind yourself that even in the midst of celebration, somewhere someone is suffering. Oh boy," he said. "I've lost my place again, and said personal things, and we were supposed to have had the second glass of wine by now. Marion, where the hell are we? All right, everybody drink."

After Sylvie and her dad left and all the dishes were washed and the candlesticks were put away, Veronica brushed her teeth and got ready for bed. The Seder resonated with her tonight in a way it never had before. She thought about the Four Children and about being capable of all kinds of behavior. This year alone she had embodied so many emotions. She had been shy. She had been daring. She had been glad. She had been miserable. She had experienced extreme love. She had been overtaken by intense grief. She had behaved badly. She had behaved heroically. She had done all this and she was just one small person.

Here, There, and Everywhere

The ceremony of Passover made way for another, which was not affiliated with any particular religious group but was known to all as Park Worship. In the first few weeks of spring when the weather was warmer spring fever arrived. The trees were full of leaves and the air was sweet with honeysuckle. Everyone in the middle school and the upper school would leave Randolf after dismissal and flee to Central Park.

Veronica and Sylvie leaned against the stone wall that separated Central Park from Fifth Avenue. The sun was bright and beat down on Veronica, making her feel like she glowed from the inside out. She opened up her Toasted Almond Good Humor bar while Sarah-Lisa and Athena and other girls were still on line to get theirs.

"We'll just go for a little while," Sylvie said.

"I'm not in the mood," Veronica said.

"Come on," Sylvie said, "we haven't even been once this

whole year." That wasn't really a fair thing to say, Veronica thought, since they hadn't been friends a whole year. And the weather hadn't even been nice for very long. She took a bite of her ice cream.

"Let's go to the closet world and talk to dead people," Veronica said.

At the mention of dead people Sarah-Lisa's ears pricked. "You talk to dead people?" she asked. She and Athena had bought their ice cream and were on their way into the park.

"Yes," Veronica said. "I talk to dead people."

"You are such a freak!" Sarah-Lisa said.

"So do I," Sylvie said, "and you know what? Not one of them misses you at all." Sarah-Lisa turned away. If Veronica didn't know better she would have sworn Athena looked back over her shoulder and smiled at her and Sylvie. Since failing their science project their friendship had been less than perfect. They had to do another project over the summer.

"Veronica, no offense," Sylvie continued, "but I feel like being outside today. In the sun. If you want to go home that's okay but I'm gonna stay in the park. I want to see the cherry blossoms." Sylvie walked through a break in the wall.

Veronica had no intention of following. The park made her sad. But Athena Mindendorfer and Sarah-Lisa Carver were nearby, and Veronica didn't want them to think she and Sylvie were fighting, so she followed Sylvie in. Runners, joggers, and high-speed walkers made loops around the reservoir, chasing physical fitness. It was bewildering. (Veronica was a Morgan through and through. None of them were exercisers.)

And then there were the dogs.

Everywhere. Dogs leaping. Dogs wagging their tails. Dogs sniffing other dogs. Dogs on the hunt for invisible prey. Dogs looking up at their owners. Dogs alive with the scent of squirrels nearby. Dogs getting to know each other by touching noses. There was such etiquette among dogs. It was so sweet, the combination of enthusiasm and gentleness. A cute dog with beagley ears came her way. She knew she shouldn't have come in here. It just made her think of Cadbury. She turned away from the beagley dog.

They followed a wide path to a grove of cherry blossoms. The branches reached out in every direction and created a canopy overhead. It was hard to tell where one tree began and another one ended. They reminded her of the poem her class had read at the beginning of the year:

O chestnut-tree, great-rooted blossomer,
Are you the leaf, the blossom or the bole?
O body swayed to music, O brightening glance,
How can we know the dancer from the dance?

On the other side of the cherry grove was a sloping meadow. Veronica spontaneously galloped down the hill and Sylvie followed. They both gathered speed and

Veronica closed her eyes until she collapsed at the bottom. It was so fun they did it again and again until they were exhausted and lay in a tangled laughing heap.

"Sylvie, I hope you don't take this the wrong way, but you are almost as fun as Cadbury when it comes to running down hills."

"Thank you," Sylvie said. They lay on their backs watching the clouds overhead. "Veronica, did you have any kind of ceremony for Cadbury?"

"Huh?"

"Like, did you pick a day and a place and remember him?" Veronica felt her mood sour.

"Sylvie, there was no day," she said. "There was every day. I cried all the time and remembered him every day."

"I'm not trying to say you didn't miss him. Gosh. I was just thinking it might be nice to have a ceremony for him here."

"In Central Park?" Veronica asked. "Now? He died months ago."

"I know. But wasn't this, like, both your favorite place?" Veronica felt like Sylvie was trying to ruin everything.

"Yeah, and I want to keep it that way," Veronica said, almost under her breath.

"After my mother died, we took her ashes to Hawaii. That's where she was born and it was always her favorite place. I remember scattering the ashes into the ocean. I didn't really understand what was happening at first. I was really little. When a breeze kicked in and all her ashes flew away, I cried. I didn't want her to go. But now I don't exactly feel like she's gone. I feel like she's just everywhere. She's in the ground I walk on. She's in the air I breathe. I miss her all the time. And I never feel alone either because she's everywhere. It's weird."

Veronica thought that made a lot of sense.

The Ceremony

Veronica and Sylvie met at ten o'clock the next Saturday morning. They chose the entrance to the park on Ninety-Eighth Street because it was located between their apartments.

The air had that grassy, fresh green smell. Veronica led them to the meadow she and Cadbury had spent the most time in and then to his favorite tree. She remembered so clearly the way he used to sniff around the roots and squat as though he was about to poop, then stand up and resume his search. Sometimes he would walk around the trunk four times before settling on the right spot. Like he only had one chance and it had to be perfect.

Veronica opened her wooden box and looked at what was left of her most special friend. She would never understand how he had become a box of remains. But she knew she was going to spread Cadbury's ashes and she knew this violet patch growing between two roots was the right place. She had searched high and low for a poem or a prayer or some way to honor him and do him justice. She had made herself hysterical, in fact, but now, watching the gray grit sift toward the ground, she felt there was nothing that needed to be said. The rain would fall, the earth would absorb his ashes, and in a matter of time Cadbury would literally become part of the tree he loved so much. He would live again as part of something else.

She and Sylvie spent the rest of the day in the park. They trekked under bridges, over hills, through cherry groves. They climbed rocks and lay in meadows. Veronica felt the same kind of thrill as when she'd first discovered the park with Cadbury. And just like with Cadbury, she was surprised at how close she could feel to another living being, this time Sylvie, when they didn't speak at all.

Mrs. Ferguson

May was making way for June and the first year of Randolf was at a close. After a nice game of Scrabble, Mary sent Veronica out to the store to buy ice cream for dessert. As Veronica walked down Fifth Avenue she encountered an exhausted-looking Mrs. Ferguson, who was still in her nightgown, albeit covered by a fur coat, as though that coat were a bathrobe. She was holding a cup of coffee in one hand and the leash of an extremely bedraggled-looking Fitzy in the other.

"Fitzy!" Veronica screamed, and fumbled with the ice cream. It was terrible. She had been so preoccupied she'd completely forgotten about Fitzy. She reminded herself of a babysitter she'd had when she was four who had come into her life like the most exciting fireworks and then just, poof, disappeared. She tried to make up for it by covering Fitzy with kisses.

Fitzy barely responded. Was she mad that Veronica had

disappeared? Or was she suffering from some medical condition? Veronica did not remember Fitzy ever looking so under the weather.

"Veronica dear," Mrs. Ferguson said, "Mr. Ferguson and I have so been wanting you to come for a visit but we didn't want to impose. Your mother told me what happened to Cadbury and we're so terribly sorry. What awful news. And now, with all hell breaking loose upstairs."

As she spoke Fitzy pooped and Mrs. Ferguson made no move to clean it up. Veronica stared at the warm blob trying not to think how it was going to end up on the bottom of someone's sneaker. She considered using the bag the ice cream was in. But that might be rude, to clean it up in front of Mrs. Ferguson. Although Mrs. Ferguson probably wouldn't even notice. She was the sort of person who only saw the things that interested her. Dog poop definitely didn't interest her.

"What's going on upstairs?" Veronica finally asked.

"Oh my word! I thought the whole building knew. We've had puppies."

New Arrivals

When Veronica and Sylvie showed up at the Ferguson apartment the following afternoon Mrs. Ferguson answered the door. She was still in her nightgown and still holding a cup of coffee. And just beyond her, lo and behold, were three of the cutest puppies Veronica had ever seen. They were running and rolling and slipping and sliding around Mr. Ferguson's leather-bound chair. The white parts of their coats were so shiny they sparkled like snowflakes. Two were solid white and had the most perfect ears. Ears that were undeniably Cadbury's. One puppy, a golden and white one with slightly shaggy hair like his mother's but his father's coloring exactly, began to lick Veronica uncontrollably the minute she picked him up. He was white except for a left caramel ear, a caramel patch on his left side, and a caramel circle above his tail. He had that same tail Cadbury had, the kind of tail that looked as though it had been dipped in a bucket of white paint.

"Three of them found homes while we were still in Miami,

but we had to come home with the others. It was just too much. Mr. Ferguson and I are desperate to get rid of the rest. They're just destroying everything!" As if on cue, another puppy came running over with a piece of Mrs. Ferguson's fur coat in its mouth.

"Oh my! Put that back! Come here!" Mrs. Ferguson yelled, chasing the speedy little pup around her living room. "Do you girls know anyone who wants puppies?"

"Um, yeah! Me," Veronica said.

"And me!" Sylvie echoed.

"You do? Isn't it too soon?" Mrs. Ferguson said. "Your parents weren't sure you were ready."

"I'm ready," Veronica said, holding the little caramel one close. She wondered if she should choose one who didn't look so much like Cadbury, but this one looked deep into her eyes. She was sure he was smiling at her. "I am so ready," she said. The puppy looked ready too.